P9-CAM-387

First American Edition 2020
Kane Miller, A Division of EDC Publishing

Text © Alesha Dixon, 2019
Cover design by Kat Godard, Dradog
Inside illustrations by Mike Love in the style of James Lancett
represented by the Bright Agency © Scholastic, 2019
The right of Alesha Dixon to be identified as
the author of this Work has been asserted by her.

First published in the UK by Scholastic Ltd., 2019
This edition published under license from Scholastic Ltd.

This is a work of fiction. Names, characters, places, incidents and
dialogues are products of the author's imagination or are used
fictitiously. Any resemblance to actual people, living or dead, events or
locales is entirely coincidental.

For information contact:
Kane Miller, A Division of EDC Publishing
PO Box 470663
Tulsa, OK 74147-0663
www.kanemiller.com
www.usbornebooksandmore.com
www.edcpub.com

Library of Congress Control Number: 2019946974
Printed and bound in the United States of America
1 2 3 4 5 6 7 8 9 10
ISBN: 978-1-68464-080-5

ALESHA DIXON

In collaboration with Katy Birchall
Illustrated by James Lancett

Kane Miller
A DIVISION OF EDC PUBLISHING

To the greatest light of all –
my mum, Beverley

1

I've always wanted to go to Buckingham Palace.

It's kind of weird that I haven't been to see it before, especially when I live close to London. But my school has never taken us there on a trip, and whenever we've come into the city as a family, we've been visiting my dad at his office in the Natural History Museum or going to the theater or attending a secret Superhero Conference underneath the Houses of Parliament or whatever. You know, totally normal stuff like that.

So, when I stepped out of the car and gazed up at the palace for the first time, I gasped in amazement and felt a shiver of excitement run down my spine. I know I've seen it on television loads of times, but Buckingham Palace is so much more breathtaking when you see it in person. It's just so *grand* and beautiful, with hundreds and hundreds of shining windows and all these tall, imposing columns.

And to think the Queen is in there! Right there, in that building! Maybe peeking out at us from behind one of those windows.

I was hit by a *huge* wave of nerves. Butterflies fluttered uncontrollably in my stomach and I felt a little bit sick. Because, unlike the tourists taking selfies in front of the palace gates, I wasn't just here to see Buckingham Palace and take some photos in front of it.

I was here to see the Queen. *And* receive a medal from her.

Me. Aurora Beam. The girl who last night hit herself in the face with her phone when she sneezed.

Here to meet the Queen.

THE QUEEN. THE ACTUAL QUEEN.

Yeah, I know. I'm not joking.

"OK, everyone," Dad gulped, frantically straightening his purple polka-dot bow tie. "Just act normal. Act completely normal. No need to panic. No need to feel nervous. No need to worry in the slightest" – his voice climbed an octave, hitting the highest pitch it has ever reached – "just be cool, everyone; be calm and collected. This is really not a big deal. We're just at a palace meeting the

3

monarch of our great nation. There is absolutely noooo need to panic. None at all. We'll go in and meet the Queen and that's that. Easy peasy, lemon squeezy."

"Henry," my mum said gently, shooting me a knowing smile, "I think we might all find it easier to relax if you weren't talking as though you'd just inhaled from a helium balloon. Just take a deep breath and calm down."

"I don't know what you're talking about!" he squeaked. "I am PERFECTLY CALM."

My friend Suzie rolled her eyes as she fiddled with the sleeve of her pretty dress. "Also, no offense, Professor Beam, I know you're like a big nerd scientist and everything, but not even true nerds like you can pull off the phrase 'easy peasy, lemon squeezy.' You need some *serious* guidance on your use of vocabulary."

"Thank you, Suzie," my grandmother, Nanny Beam, chuckled, checking her bright-pink hair in a compact mirror. "I'm glad someone pointed that out. I was just about to say the same thing."

As everyone stifled giggles, a man wearing a smart black tailcoat and a red vest with gold buttons emerged from a door in one of the archways and stepped across the gravel toward us.

"The Beams!"

He grinned, stopping in front of us and bowing his head slightly. His eyes flickered down to my dog, Kimmy, who sat at my feet. I'd taken her to the groomers the day before especially for the occasion and Mum had tied a shiny red bow around her neck, so she looked her absolute best for the Queen.

"And Kimmy, of course," the butler continued, smiling warmly at her. She barked happily in acknowledgement. "Welcome to Buckingham Palace. My name is Joe and I'll be showing you the way to the ceremony, so please do follow me and let's get out of this freezing cold and into the warmth."

Thanks to the adrenaline pumping at a hundred miles per hour through my veins, I hadn't even noticed the cold, but now that he'd mentioned it, I realized I could barely feel my hands. It was a gray, bitterly cold day. Christmas was only a couple of weeks away and snowfall was expected in England any day now, according to the news.

Joe led the way and we all followed in a line, like a row of ducklings, and as he held open the door for us, he announced, "I know this isn't very professional, but I am SO excited to have been chosen to take you to the Palace Ballroom." He paused and looked directly at me. "Aurora Beam – or would you rather go by your hero name, Lightning Girl? – I can't believe I'm meeting a real *superhero*."

"Not just one," I pointed out.

"Ah, yes." He nodded enthusiastically at Mum, misunderstanding what I meant. "I'm a huge fan of yours too, Mrs. Beam."

"Thank you," Mum said, catching my eye. "But I'm not the one receiving a medal today. These superheroes right here are." She gestured to my group of friends, standing beside me. "The Bright Sparks."

A warm smile spread across Joe's face. "Of course. What an honor to meet the famous

7

Bright Sparks!" He began leading the way down the corridor, turning to Georgie who fell into step with him. "Any chance on the way you can tell me about your latest adventure?"

As Georgie launched into her telling of the story, I gazed up in awe at the magnificent gold-framed paintings lining our way and thought about how on EARTH we had ended up here.

When I first found out I had superpowers, I'd never have imagined that my friends and I would form a superhero club called the Bright Sparks, come face-to-face with a real-life bad guy several times, land ourselves in *serious* danger and then end up at Buckingham Palace to receive a medal from the Queen. I can't believe it has almost been a year since I accidentally destroyed the garden because light beams blasted uncontrollably from my hands, and Mum and Dad sat me down to tell me that all the women in my family have superpowers and have for centuries. My mum wasn't a businesswoman with a boring office job like I'd thought. She was a superhero and now I had developed the powers to become one, too. It had been a lot to take in.

And a whole lot more has happened since then.

Kizzy has always been my best friend but, back then, I barely spoke to Georgie, Suzie and Fred. That was because we are all so *different*. Fred is the class joker; Georgie, the most fashionable and stylish girl in school; Suzie is super sporty, the best at gymnastics and likes to be the center of attention; Kizzy is quiet and intelligent and would love to read all day; and I ... well, I'm not the best at anything and just wanted to stay out of everyone's way.

But when they witnessed my superpowers, they decided to band together to form the

Bright Sparks so that I wouldn't have to face any adventures alone. They would bring all their special qualities, just like I brought mine. It's worked, too.

Without the Bright Sparks sticking together, we would never have stopped the notorious Blackout Burglar, who had been posing as Mr. Mercury, a science teacher at our school. He had been plotting to steal the most precious stone in existence, the Light of the World (which happens to be the source of all the Beam family powers), from the Natural History Museum.

But even though we saved it from being stolen that time in the museum, we weren't able to stop it from being stolen from the global gathering of superheroes beneath the Houses of Parliament last summer. Mr. Mercury had been under my nose all that time, in another disguise. He fooled all of us.

And he wasn't the only one who had us fooled.

"Hello? Earth to Aurora!"

I jolted at Kizzy's voice.

"Are you OK?" she said, raising her eyebrow at me. "You've fallen quite far behind."

I'd been so lost in my thoughts that I hadn't even noticed that the others were ahead, disappearing around a corner. If Kizzy hadn't waited, Kimmy and I might have gotten lost in the maze of Buckingham Palace.

"Oh, yeah, I'm fine." I smiled, picking up the pace with Kimmy trotting elegantly next to me on her leash. She had obviously completely understood when I'd asked her to be on her best behavior and, no matter what, to PLEASE not go to the bathroom *inside* the palace.

"What were you thinking about?" Kizzy asked, looking very pretty in her blue-lace, high-neck dress. It was nice seeing everyone all dressed up and Georgie had even designed and ordered special gold lightning-bolt pins for us all to wear.

I gestured to the red carpet we were currently walking along. "I was thinking about all this. How we got here. It feels like a long time ago when you worked out that Mr. Mercury was going to try and rob the Natural History Museum and steal the Light of the World for his boss."

She nodded thoughtfully as we turned the corner and began to catch up with the others.

"Weird, isn't it? Being here, I mean. Do you think the Queen will talk to us? Ask us questions?" she said, glancing at me nervously.

I shrugged. "You know more about this sort of thing than me. Didn't you read a book on it or something?"

"I read five. One on the history of Buckingham Palace, one on its artwork collection, a biography of the Queen, a book on royal etiquette and behavior and, well" – she paused, the corner of her mouth twitching into a smile – "one on the palace dogs."

"*Very* helpful in this situation, I'm sure." I laughed.

"I read it on Kimmy's behalf! You never know, it might come in useful. What happens if Kimmy needs to be introduced to one of the pets here? At least I'll know who's who."

"That's it," I giggled, shaking my head. "You've officially lost your mind."

"It's not my fault." Kizzy sighed. "I've just been SO nervous. The Queen, Aurora! Meeting me! I feel like I don't deserve to be here."

"Trust me," I whispered as we came to a halt in front of some grand, gold-leafed doors. "You *definitely* deserve to be here."

Kizzy squeezed my hand. The butler gently reminded Suzie that unfortunately, as he mentioned before, she really wasn't allowed to practice cartwheels down the long corridors despite how perfect they would be for such a display, and then opened the doors and stepped aside to let us through.

The Buckingham Palace ballroom was the most magnificent room I've ever seen. It was so elegant. It had a pristine red-and-gold carpet, beautiful watercolor paintings on the walls in heavy gold frames and glittering chandeliers hanging from the ceiling. Another butler welcomed us to the room and showed us to our row as everyone waited for the Queen to arrive. The rest of the Bright Sparks spotted their parents, who were already in their seats, and waved to them, pretending not to notice that the room had erupted into an excited ripple of whispers when we walked in.

"My hands are *very* sweaty," Fred said, as I patted my lightning-bolt pin to check that it was safely attached to my dress.

"Ew, Fred. Thanks for that information." Suzie wrinkled her nose. "You're so gross."

"All right, you two." Nanny Beam chuckled. "No bickering. The Queen will be here any minute."

"I hope they take lots of photos," Mum said, watching the official photographers getting their cameras ready. "I'm going to frame every single one of the Bright Sparks receiving their medals. Henry, we'll have to move all your science books off the shelves to make room for all the new frames we'll be getting. It's about time you had a clear-out."

Dad looked horrified and opened his mouth to say something, but there was a sudden trumpet fanfare, the doors at the end of the room opened and in walked the Queen.

The Queen.

My breath caught in my throat and I closed my eyes and pinched my wrist just in case I was actually dreaming. But when I opened my eyes I was still there, in the ballroom of Buckingham Palace, and the Queen was right in front of me, smiling at us, her eyes twinkling.

This. Was. Surreal.

Mum reached over and took my hand as a lump formed in my throat.

"Enjoy every moment," she whispered. "I'm so proud of you, Aurora."

The next half an hour became a wonderful, hazy blur as our achievements were all read out individually before we were asked to each step up and receive our medals from the Queen. I was so overwhelmed by excitement and nerves, I can barely remember standing in front of her as she gave me my medal with a warm smile, congratulating me and saying she looked forward to having a chat after the ceremony. I can't even remember walking back to my seat, but I somehow must have done.

"She asked me whether I'd considered designing accessories for the royal family as a future career!" Georgie exclaimed afterward, as we enjoyed a cup of tea. "Then she said she liked the lightning-bolt sunglasses I'd designed for you, Aurora, and asked where she could get a pair! The Queen wants a pair of sunglasses designed by me! Can you believe it?"

"I can," Kizzy said as she nodded. "Your designs are amazing!"

"It comes as no surprise to any of us that she'd want you on her accessory team, Georgie!" Dad smiled, putting an arm around Mum. "We're so proud of all of you. You looked great up there."

"What did she say when you collected yours, Suzie?" Mum asked as Suzie gazed adoringly at her medal.

"That she looked forward to seeing me win my first gold medal one day as part of the Olympic Team GB," Suzie gushed, her cheeks flushing with glee. "I told her it wouldn't be long."

"Nothing can beat what she said to me, I reckon," Fred said smugly.

"Oh, yeah?" Suzie raised her eyebrows.

"Yeah," he said firmly. "She gave me a little tip."

"A tip about what?"

He grinned. "About the best prank she's ever played on someone."

Suzie's eyes widened in disbelief. "The *Queen* told you about a prank she's played?"

"That's right," he said, taking a large bite from his slice of cake. "And it was hilarious. She's a real genius."

As Suzie began trying to get him to spill the beans on this prank, I felt a tap on my shoulder and turned to find a butler standing behind me.

"Miss Beam, the Queen would like a private audience with you in a separate room of the palace. Please follow me."

"Me?" I asked. "The Queen wants to see me? Are you sure?"

He smiled. "Quite sure. When you're ready, I will take you to her."

I did as I was told, tripping over my feet as I followed him out of the room, down a corridor and toward another set of doors. I felt dizzy with nerves and wished that I had asked Mum or Dad to come with me.

My brain was fuzzy with questions. What was happening? Why on earth would she want to talk to me in private? And did I have to curtsy again? Was it the left foot or the right foot that tucks behind when you curtsy? Or do I bow? What do I do with my hands? And what do I call her? Your Majesty? Ma'am? Do I sit? Do I stand?

WHY DIDN'T I READ FIVE BOOKS ABOUT THIS LIKE KIZZY?

By the time we reached the doors, where several security men and women were standing, my palms were clammy enough to give Fred a run for his money and I couldn't remember one word of the English language.

"Ah, Miss Beam. Do come in," the Queen said, as the doors opened to reveal her, in a small, cozy room with a large fireplace, sitting on a red velvet chair and sipping a cup of tea. There were more members of security in the room, standing out of the way by the windows and in the corners. If I wasn't so nervous and if the Queen hadn't been in  the room, I would have asked for selfies with them because they all looked like they'd just stepped off the set of a James Bond movie.

I tripped over my feet again – WHY did I decide to wear these shoes?! – and then attempted a clumsy curtsy when I got closer to her.

"No need for all that," she smiled, with a wave of her hand. "Please, do sit down. I imagine you're wondering why you're here?"

I nodded, too nervous to speak.

"I look forward to joining the recipients of all the medals in just a moment, but before I do, I wanted to have a quick word with you, Aurora." She put her china cup and saucer down and rested her hands in her lap. Her eyes were so kind and her aura so relaxed, I began to feel a little more at ease, despite the fact I could see a security man in the corner of my eye touching his earpiece every now and then. "I'm very grateful to you for all that you have done for us. It's not every day a twelve-year-old achieves such feats of bravery. You should be very proud of yourself. I certainly am."

"Th–thank you," I managed to croak.

"I would like to tell you something very important," she said in a more serious tone, her eyes holding mine. "You see, there is something that you need to know. I think... yes, I think it is time you knew the truth."

She paused and picked up her teacup again. I stared at her, with absolutely no idea what was going on.

What important truth could the Queen possibly want to tell ... *me*?

"But before I tell you, I would like to hear your story."

"My ... my story?"

"Yes. I would like you to tell me all the events of the past few weeks that led up to you being here today."

I hesitated, wondering if this was another prank, like the one she'd told Fred about. But she was looking at me perfectly seriously.

And when the Queen asks you to tell her your story, you tell her your story.

"I guess it all started at the end of summer vacation." I gulped. "When I got into a little bit of trouble. . ."

Her eyes twinkled mischievously.

"That sounds like my favorite kind of story," she said. "Start from the beginning."

2

Four Months Earlier

I was in trouble. Big trouble.

To be precise, I was in prison.

This was all just one big misunderstanding. I kept saying that to the officer as she led me into the police station, but she ignored me, even though I was explaining myself very clearly. I had to fill out all this paperwork and then she asked me to write a statement of "my version of events," giving me a very suspicious look as she said it. Except my statement wasn't *my version of events*, it was the absolute TRUTH. And anybody in my position would have done exactly the same.

You know, if someone actually *told* me what was going on once in a while then none of this would have happened. The whole reason I'd gotten myself into this mess in the first place was because I was being kept completely in the dark. It was the end of summer vacation, the new school term was just about to start, and the Light of the World was still *missing*.

And we didn't seem to be any closer to finding it.

The Light of the World was not only the source of our family's superpowers, but it was also the most precious stone on the planet. We had no idea where it was or who had it or what they wanted to do with it. It could be anywhere on Earth.

What if whoever had it intended to destroy it? Would my superpowers just ... *disappear*? Would something bad happen to me? And Mum? And my grandmother and aunt, who also had powers?

Not knowing why someone would want the Light of the World and what they were planning to do with it made me feel sick. It wasn't just my family in trouble if it landed in the wrong hands, it was the *whole world* too. We didn't fully understand how powerful that stone was yet – and it was very likely that the person who had it wasn't planning to use it for good, considering they'd stolen it at the Superhero Conference.

We *had* to get it back safe and sound.

All we knew was that the criminal mastermind who was behind stealing the stone from right under our noses during the summer was the same person who had tried to steal it from the Natural History Museum last spring, and whoever they were, they had employed Mr. Mercury both times to do their dirty work. This meant that Mr. Mercury was the key to finding the Light of the World.

"I know, Aurora, don't worry; we're doing everything we can to track down Mr. Mercury," Mum kept saying in a tired voice every time I reminded her just how bad this situation was and pestered her for an update.

She refused to tell me any more than that, so can anyone blame me for trying to take things into my own hands? This was a BIG deal and, in my opinion, everyone was acting WAY too calm.

I kept calling Nanny Beam in Cornwall about five times a day to see if she had any updates, but she was even cagier than Mum. Not that I should have been surprised, considering her job. After the Superhero Conference, we'd all found out that Nanny Beam didn't just run a rescue sanctuary for animals in Cornwall but also happened to be head of MI5, with a secret underground lair in her house and a bright-pink flying car.

It had been quite the revelation.

Personally, I thought it was *awesome*. How many people can say that their grandmother is a spy? But I can kind of see why Mum was still weirded out by the whole thing. She'd thought that Nanny Beam was retired and chilling with rescue alpacas and chickens in Cornwall, while Mum had taken over saving the world from bad guys. But Nanny Beam had secretly been keeping an eye on her all the time, anonymously sending her on rescue missions for years. Mum was still trying to get her head round it.

On top of all that, we'd gained a new family member at the same time. Darek Vermore, one of the most famous and successful technological businessmen in the world, turned out to be the only son of Nanny Beam's brother, Nolan.

Yeah. Darek Vermore was Mum's *cousin*.

I never met Nolan or knew all that much about him because he died when my mum was a teenager, and then he was hardly mentioned when we were growing up. Nanny Beam had a big falling-out with him right before he died and, according to Mum, she didn't like to talk about it. It was too painful. When I was staying at Nanny Beam's house in Cornwall during the summer I found an old photograph of Nanny Beam, her brother and a young boy. It was nice because I'd never seen what my great-uncle Nolan looked like before.

Then, with the excitement of the Superhero Conference, I forgot all about the picture until Nanny Beam revealed that Mr. Vermore was her nephew and I suddenly realized he was the young boy in that photo. Nanny Beam told us that even though she'd fallen out with his dad, Darek had stayed in touch and then they'd ended up working together.

I keep meaning to ask Nanny Beam what had happened to make her fall out with her brother in the first place, but it never seems to be the right time.

Anyway, before all these crazy family secrets came spilling out, I had thought it was strange that Mr. Vermore, a non-superhero, was in charge of the Superhero Conference and it was held in the building he'd designed underneath the Houses of Parliament. I'd even become suspicious that he might be the one trying to steal the Light of the World. But obviously now that I know he is Nanny Beam's nephew and had been working alongside her to *protect* the precious stone, I feel a bit guilty about suspecting him.

Although, to be fair, he thought *I* was the one who'd stolen it, so I guess we're even.

My older brother, Alexis, couldn't have been happier about our new family member. A big computer nerd, Alexis worshipped Darek Vermore, and ever since we'd discovered we were related, Alexis wouldn't shut up about him. My little sister, Clara, and I were constantly rolling our eyes at him because he always managed to bring Darek into any conversation.

"Why don't you just call him and ask for a chat? Maybe he could give you work experience at his company or something," Clara had said when Alexis had spent about half an hour reeling off Darek's many achievements.

Alexis's eyes had grown as wide as saucers. "I can't just pick up the phone and *call* Darek Vermore! He's *Darek Vermore*!"

"Sure you can," I'd said. "He's family."

"You don't get it," he'd said, shaking his head. "You just don't get it. He is an ICON."

He was absolutely right. Clara and I didn't get it at all. Our brother was a big weirdo.

The thing was, I really believed that after Mr. Mercury sped away into the distance, slipping through our clutches, it would only be a matter of time before we caught him again. I mean, HELLO, my grandmother was head of MI5! And her nephew happened to own the biggest tech company in the country! He was literally in charge of developing and manufacturing the most advanced spy equipment out there.

There was NO chance Mr. Mercury could escape for too long.

But he had. He was nowhere to be seen and neither was the Light of the World. And no one would tell me anything. So, I had been doing what anyone in my position would and spending all my spare time trawling through social media and online news reports for any sign of Mr. Mercury or any clues that might lead us to the Light of the World.

At one point, there was some weird light phenomenon going on over Jamaica – witnesses had seen the northern lights appear in the sky there. It HAD to be linked to the Light of the World. It just had to be. It was in Jamaica! So, I asked Mum what we were going to do about it and she just said the same thing she always did.

"Don't worry, Aurora, we're handling it.

Now, have you got the list of textbooks we need to get you for the new school year?"

WHAT WAS WRONG WITH HER?

Who cares about *textbooks* at a time like this? Had she lost her mind?! As soon as she brushed me off, I went straight online and booked flights to Jamaica using Dad's credit card. And OK, yes, sneaking his credit card from his wallet was maybe wrong, but this was important!

They both got really angry at me when I appeared at the bottom of the stairs with our passports and the boarding passes printed out, announcing that we had to leave now or we'd miss our plane. Dad's eyes almost bulged right out of his head when he saw the price of the flights and he got straight on the phone to the airline to try and get a refund, while Mum said in a very strained manner that we "needed to have a little chat."

Apparently, Nanny Beam had already sent

agents to Jamaica and nothing had been found. If the stone had been there, it had been moved somewhere else now.

But that was all Mum's fault because if she'd just told me that in the first place, I never would have felt the need to take a trip to Jamaica into my own hands.

It was my birthday the day after the flights fiasco and I was worried that Mum was still going to be mad, but luckily she wasn't. The Bright Sparks came round, and we had an amazing pink, yellow and purple lightning bolt cake that Dad had spent ages making. Suzie said it was the best cake she'd ever tasted, which is really something. And when I quietly apologized to Mum about nabbing the credit card and booking the flights, she just put her arm around me.

"Don't worry about it, I know you were doing what you thought was right," she'd said gently. "And anyway, it's your birthday! That means everything is forgiven."

It was a very nice moment.

Unfortunately, I had a feeling she might not be so forgiving about this whole prison thing.

I was only trying to help. I was scrolling through Twitter like I did every morning, searching for the words "Mercury" or "blackout

burglar," and among all the tweets discussing his crimes was a sighting. An actual *sighting*.

@Unicorn245

Pretty sure that I've just seen that dude wanted

by police, Mr. Mercury, lurking in Broxbourne

Woods. He's shorter than I imagined. Called the

police *#MrMercury #LightningGirl*

I almost fell off my chair. Broxbourne Woods! That's in Hertfordshire, where we live! He was so close! I didn't even hesitate. I ran downstairs to tell Mum and Dad, but I only found Alexis on his laptop and Clara lying on the floor next to a contentedly snoozing Kimmy, reading one of her new science textbooks.

"Where are Mum and Dad?" I asked urgently.

"Out," Alexis replied, not looking up from his laptop.

"Out *where*?"

He shrugged.

"UGH!" I cried out in frustration and ran back up the stairs to get my phone, calling a taxi straightaway.

I left the house, yelling behind me to Alexis and Clara that I would be back soon, climbed into the taxi and was driven at high speed toward Broxbourne Woods, my hands shaking in anticipation. I thought about letting the Bright Sparks know what was going on, but there wasn't time for them to all get here and I didn't want to risk waiting around and giving Mr. Mercury the time to escape. I'd have to handle this myself.

When I got to the woodland, I realized that I didn't really know where to start. The woods were big, and he could be anywhere. So I followed the path for a bit, weaving through the trees, staying as quiet as possible and keeping my eyes peeled.

That's when I saw him.

At first, I just saw a glint of light among the trees, but then I realized it was the sunlight reflecting off a big round bald head. Mr. Mercury. He had his back to me and a satchel hanging from his shoulder. I couldn't believe how lucky I was to have come across him so easily. I quickly called the police and told them that I could confirm that their earlier caller was correct, Mr. Mercury was in Broxbourne Woods.

"We have officers on their way. Please go back to the entrance to the woods and wait safely for them to arrive," the operator said.

"No, don't worry, I've got this," I said confidently.

"What? Wait! Miss, you need to—"

But I hung up, conscious I was wasting time. At any moment, Mr. Mercury might notice he wasn't alone. I tiptoed toward him, holding my breath, careful not to step on any cracking twigs. I knew that I wouldn't be able to hold him by myself before the police got there, but I could take his bag, which might have important information or even the Light of the World in it. And when the police got there, they could capture him.

I waited until I was close enough and then I held out my hands and I focused.

I hadn't used my powers since the last time I'd tried to stop Mr. Mercury, outside the Houses of Parliament a week before, after the Superhero Conference. I closed my eyes and concentrated on that warm, tingling feeling running up from my toes as though sparklers were going off through my veins.

Suddenly, dazzling light beams burst from my palms, bathing the woodland in a bright light and catching Mr. Mercury off guard.

He yelped, shielding his eyes, and I pounced, knowing this was my only chance to have the

upper hand.

I snatched his bag from round his shoulder and before he even knew what was going on, I sprinted away from him as fast as I could.

"STOP! THIEF!"

I kept running, hearing his footsteps close behind me, but I was much faster, taking random turnings round trees, darting left and right to throw him off the scent. When I was certain that he wasn't in close pursuit, I hid behind a wide tree trunk and, catching my breath, I tore open the bag and looked inside.

"Huh?"

There was a pair of binoculars and . . . a book on British birds? It didn't make any sense.

Obviously, *now* I know that it made perfect sense. Because it wasn't Mr. Mercury. It was a bird-watcher. He just had a bald head. And I'd attacked him and stolen his bag with no explanation.

Whoops.

In my defense, the person who tweeted about spotting Mr. Mercury in Broxbourne Woods should really have checked that it really *was* Mr. Mercury before they told the Internet about it. And as soon as I realized my mistake, I gave the bag right back and apologized maybe a thousand times to the random bald bird-watcher.

Unfortunately, by that time the police had arrived, and I was driven back to the station with the siren on and everything.

It was actually quite cool.

Mum arrived to pick me up from prison with a face like thunder. Dad was with her and kept whispering, "It was just a misunderstanding, Kiyana, she didn't know," while she pursed her lips and ordered me to get into the car. Matters weren't exactly helped when some of the police officers asked for selfies with me before I left. Mum's eyes narrowed to slits as she told them that under no circumstances could they take any photos of Lightning Girl right now, and the police officer in charge stepped forward to assure her that, as per their agreement, this "incident" would not become public knowledge.

We sat in silence as Dad drove us home until, eventually, Mum spoke through gritted teeth.

"Luckily, the bird-watcher has decided not to press charges and he's agreed to keep the story to himself. It turns out he's a big fan of Lightning Girl and can understand the ...

mix-up," she said, staring straight ahead.

"Great!" I said. "That's good news."

Silence.

"So," I began, "how's your day been?"

I realize now that this was probably a bit too flippant a question.

"How's our day been?" Mum hissed, swiveling to look at me. "I just picked up my twelve-year-old daughter from a *police station*.

Do you have any idea what you've put us through? How worried we were when we got a call from the police to say our daughter had committed THEFT?"

"I told you what happened! I was just trying to help!" I

argued. "The Light of the World is out there, and we haven't gotten any closer to finding it! I wanted to do something!"

Dad reached over and put a hand on one of Mum's. She took a deep breath and her voice was softer when she spoke.

"I know, Aurora. I know you were just trying to help. But" – she swiveled to face me again – "you *must* start trusting us. We are doing everything we can to find the Light of the World. The best people are on the job and just because it doesn't look like anything is going on, it doesn't mean that's the case. It's very important work and a lot of it is top secret. Not even Dad or I know a lot about what is happening. That's how MI5 works. You just have to trust that everything that can be done *is* being done. Will you do that for me?"

I let out a long sigh. "I guess."

"Good. Aurora, this is important. I want you

to promise that you will stop looking for Mr. Mercury and the Light of the World."

"But, Mum! The Bright Sparks and I can help! We've shown that we can—"

"Yes, the Bright Sparks have been amazing and stopped Mr. Mercury several times. But it's bigger now," Mum said firmly as Dad nodded in agreement with her. "It's more dangerous. We don't know who is pulling the strings or what they're capable of. Your safety, the Bright Sparks' safety, comes first. It's my job to protect you. As soon as you need to know anything, or you can help in some way, I will talk to you straightaway. OK?"

I stared out the window and didn't say anything.

"Aurora, I need you to promise me you will stop looking for Mr. Mercury and the Light of the World."

"But—"

"Aurora," she said sternly. "Promise me."

I lifted my eyes to meet hers.

"I promise," I said quietly.

She smiled, satisfied, and said we could all forget about my arrest before changing the subject. She had no idea that the whole time I had my fingers crossed behind my back.

3

"They're trying to kill me."

Fred slumped forward onto the table, knocking over his water glass so that it flooded his lunch tray.

"Who is trying to kill you?" Kizzy asked, passing him a spare napkin.

"The teachers!" he cried in exasperation. "They're all in it together! It's the first week back at school and already I'm behind. Aren't we allowed to have *any* fun anymore? I haven't even had time to play a joke on Suzie."

"That's not true," Georgie corrected. "You covered everything in her locker with tinfoil two days ago."

A smile spread across his face as he remembered. "Oh, yeah. Classic."

"It was *not* classic," Suzie huffed. "And it was NOT funny. It took me forever to get all that tinfoil off my stuff. You wrapped it round every individual pen in my pencil case."

"Well, I wasn't going to do it half-heartedly,

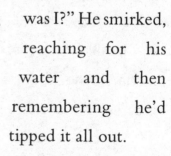

was I?" He smirked, reaching for his water and then remembering he'd tipped it all out.

"And you put those horrible toy snakes in my gymnastics bag," Suzie sniffed, folding her arms.

"True, true." Fred nodded, looking pleased with himself. "I guess for one week back at school, that's not too bad. Room for improvement, though."

Suzie narrowed her eyes at him. "Don't you dare. I've got to be focused on gymnastics at the moment. There's a big competition at the end of term and I'm planning on winning it."

"Who else would win it?" Georgie said proudly, causing Suzie to blush slightly. "You're the best in the school."

"Thanks, Georgie. I've still got a lot of practice to do, though. It's going to be a busy term."

"I can't believe this time last week we were in Cornwall," Georgie sighed. "I want to go back in time and be Sun Gazing on Nanny Beam's roof."

"And I want to go back to practicing my karate moves on Fred under Nanny Beam's instruction," Suzie said, shooting him a glare as he stuck his tongue out at her.

"I didn't get even halfway through my summer reading list," Kizzy said. "If we could only have a couple more weeks of vacation."

We all nodded collectively, although I felt as though I was on a different wavelength. The rest of the Bright Sparks might be longing for vacation, so they could read more books or squeeze in more sunshine, but I wished for more time to be able to track down Mr. Mercury and the Light of the World.

"Um, Lightning Girl?" a high-pitched voice behind me said.

I turned around to see a group of boys and girls from the year below, huddled together nervously, holding their phones.

"We were wondering whether we could get a photo with you?" a girl at the front of the group asked hopefully.

"Sure," I said, standing up from the table.

"I'll take it," Georgie offered, although she may have regretted that decision when eight phones were thrust in her face. I stood in the middle and they all gathered around me excitedly.

"All right," Georgie said, once she'd gotten the first phone ready. "Everybody, smile!"

My jaw was aching when the last photo had been taken and the phone passed back to its owner. I thanked them when they said they were my biggest fans and slid back into my seat as they rushed out of the canteen, giggling.

"The fame thing hasn't died down yet, then?" Kizzy grinned. "Are you in control of your superpowers today or do we all need to duck underneath the table?"

At the beginning of the summer, I'd become a bit overwhelmed by all the attention I was receiving because my superpowers were no longer a secret and I was known to the whole world as Lightning Girl. I got too caught up in it and ended up on the sofa of *Good Morning, Britain*, where I lost control of my powers on live TV because I was so exhausted. I sent Piers Morgan and Susannah Reid flying backward over their sofa and broke several cameras with the force of my light beams.

Needless to say, I haven't been invited back on morning television.

"Very funny." I smiled. "And no, the fame thing hasn't died down all that much. Although at least there are no reporters outside my door these days."

"You gained a whole new fan base after using your powers outside the Houses of Parliament when we were trying to stop Mr. Mercury, though," Georgie pointed out, shaking the ketchup bottle. "I've never seen your powers that ... dazzling before. It was like seeing lightning super close-up."

"Imagine if your fans knew about your stint in prison," Fred snickered. "Now, THAT would be a good headline. I can see it now: *Lightning Girl Locked Up!*"

"Shush!" Suzie hissed, jabbing him in the ribs with her pointy manicured fingernail. "You *know* no one's allowed to know about that."

"I know, I know," he said. "I still think it's the coolest thing EVER. Aurora, you are officially my favorite superhero."

"I told you, Fred, I was only held there for an hour," I said, rolling my eyes. "And you know it was just a big misunderstanding."

"I've never known anyone with a criminal past," he enthused.

"I do not have a criminal past," I insisted, but he ignored me.

"I can't believe I have a friend who's a felon,"

he said excitedly, picking up his fork and digging into his pasta. "What was prison really *like*?"

I shook my head. "I'm not telling you anything more than I've already told you. I'd rather forget about it, thank you very much."

"It's hilarious that you thought a bird-watcher was Mr. Mercury," Fred sniggered. "What would he be doing in some woodland in Hertfordshire?"

"He may have been burying the Light of the World there," I said defensively. "You never know. And, anyway, speaking of Mr. Mercury – Kizzy, have you managed to do any more research into his background as the Blackout Burglar? Any new clues?"

Kizzy looked at me guiltily. "Sorry, Aurora, I've been so busy this week with the extra classes I'm taking after school. They've let me study a few more subjects than normal.

With that and homework, I just haven't had the time."

"Don't worry, you can lend me the books if you like and I'll see if anything new jumps out at me," I offered. "Maybe he had an old hangout that he's still using today."

The others shared a look but didn't say anything.

"What?" I frowned. "What is it?"

Kizzy shifted in her seat as the rest of the Bright Sparks all looked to her to answer. "It's just, you've already gotten in quite a bit of trouble trying to track down Mr. Mercury and your parents made you promise that you would leave it to the experts now."

"Yeah, but I wasn't being serious. Wait a minute" – I glanced across their faces – "you think we should give up?"

"No! Of course not," Kizzy said hurriedly. "And we're first and foremost the Bright

Sparks, always here for you when you need us. But just remember that Nanny Beam and the whole of the British Secret Service is looking for Mr. Mercury, alongside Darek Vermore. If anyone is going to find him and track down the Light of the World, it will be them."

"They'll find them," Georgie said confidently. "There's nothing Nanny Beam can't do."

"Right." I nodded, even though I had a sinking feeling in my stomach.

I didn't want to just sit around and wait. I wanted to do something. Anything. They didn't get it. I guess I felt connected to the Light of the World in a way that they couldn't.

And the truth was, I felt largely responsible for what had happened at the Superhero Conference. How had I not recognized Mr. Mercury in disguise? I should have seen through the pretend assistant David Donnelly straightaway. And how did I let him get away when I'm the one with superpowers and he's not? If Mum had been there, he never would have been able to slip through her fingers. She's a truly amazing superhero.

But I couldn't stop him. Lightning Girl, a famous superhero, the one who everyone at school wanted pictures with, couldn't stop a jewel thief operating right under her nose.

Now, my family was in danger because *I'd* let him get away.

I couldn't sit around, do nothing and let them fix my mistakes. I had to help.

"Can we *please* talk about Paris?" Suzie said, swiftly changing the topic. "I can't believe we have to wait until after break to go! I want to go now!"

"It is going to be the best school trip ever," Fred declared. "I'm going to eat so much I won't be able to move."

"How inspiring," Suzie muttered.

"The food will be amazing, but I'm more excited about the sights," Kizzy chipped in, her eyes widening at the thought. "There is so much culture in Paris, I don't know how the teachers are possibly going to cram it all into our itinerary."

"I just want to go to the fashion houses," Georgie sighed dreamily. "Paris is the true home of Chanel."

"Are you excited about the school trip, Aurora?" Kizzy asked.

"Yeah, course," I said, as enthusiastically as I could muster. I had completely forgotten that it was even happening. "Paris. I can't wait."

*

When Dad picked Alexis, Clara and me up from school later that day, I was still thinking about our conversation at lunch. I knew that the Bright Sparks cared a lot about finding the Light of the World and discovering the identity of the mastermind behind its disappearance, but I couldn't get my head round how they were getting so involved in normal, everyday stuff, when all this was going on.

"And what about you, Aurora?" Dad said suddenly, catching my eye in the rearview mirror.

"Um, sorry, what was the question?"

"How are you finding the first week back at school?"

"Fine."

"Whoa," Alexis snorted. "Don't ramble on too much, Aurora. We don't need to hear every detail."

"Thank you for that, Alexis," Dad said, shooting him a look as we pulled up to the house.

"Hey," Clara said, looking out the window, her eyebrows knitted together, "whose car is that?"

Sitting in our driveway was the biggest, shiniest limo I'd ever seen. Alexis immediately turned in the front seat to look at me.

"Are you going on a TV breakfast show again or something?"

I shook my head. "No. I don't know anything about this."

We scrambled out of the car as soon as Dad parked on the road, curious to know who was in our house. I spotted our nosy neighbors, Mr. and Mrs. Crow, looking at our driveway through a telescope from their bedroom window. Dad pretended not to notice them as he found his keys in his pocket and opened the front door, ushering us inside.

"We're home!"

"In the kitchen!" Mum called back. "And we have a guest."

Darek Vermore stood up when we came in from the hallway and extended a hand out to shake Dad's. Four security men with earpieces were standing in the kitchen, all wearing dark sunglasses and suits. They looked very serious.

"Hello, everyone," Darek said cheerily. "How was school?"

Before anyone could answer, I stepped forward

excitedly. "Are you here with some news? Did Nanny Beam send you? Have you found the Light of the World?"

"No," he said, glancing at Mum. His gaze shifted from me to my brother. "I'm actually here about Alexis."

Dad turned to Alexis and sighed.

"What have you done now?"

"Nothing!" Alexis hesitated. "Unless this is something to do with that tiny hitch with the CIA?"

Darek chuckled and shook his head. "No, nothing to do with that. And, actually, Alexis hasn't done anything wrong; quite the opposite. I'm here with a proposition."

"What do you mean *tiny hitch with the CIA?*" Dad asked, rounding on Alexis.

"Dad, can't you see Mr. Vermore is in the middle of telling us something important?" Alexis replied hurriedly. "This is hardly the time to discuss a very *minor* incident that almost certainly did not happen."

Clara caught my eye and we both smirked. A technological genius with no respect for rules, Alexis was always getting in trouble. He had hacked into the school system loads of times to change his grades or cause chaos with the teachers, like that time he accessed all their email accounts and sent messages to other teachers, pretending to be them.

That weirdly turned out quite well because two of the teachers received love notes from one another and, although the messages turned out to be part of Alexis's prank, those particular teachers did in fact have a crush on one another. They admitted it due to the fake emails and now they're engaged.

Alexis claimed he had seen the spark between them and did it on purpose, but that didn't save him from getting a week's detention.

Anyway, when Nanny Beam let him explore the underground lair below her Cornwall cottage, which contained the most advanced MI5 tech equipment in the country, he waited until she wasn't supervising him and then he sent a notification to all members of Parliament saying not to ask questions, but that it was absolutely mandatory to national security that they all arrive at work the next day wearing pajamas.

It was all over the news when all these serious MPs turned up to the Houses of Parliament in their nighties and flannel pajama bottoms and slippers. Alexis didn't stop laughing for days.

So, it shouldn't really come as a surprise to Dad that Alexis has had a run-in with the CIA.

"I wanted to talk to Alexis about an

opportunity at Vermore Enterprises," Darek said, taking the mug of tea that Mum handed him.

"Vermore Enterprises?" Alexis gasped, stepping forward eagerly.

"Yes, that's right. You know the tagline, of course?" Darek smiled, raising his eyebrows.

"*Vermore: for people who want more*," we all chorused.

Darek burst out laughing, offering Clara a high five. "Very good! I'm pleased you've all been paying attention to those commercials. Personally, I find them deeply irritating, but my publicity department tell me they work wonders for brand recognition."

Mum opened the cookie tin to offer one to Darek with his tea, which he graciously accepted. The sound of the cookie tin being opened had been picked up by Kimmy, who had been busy outside protecting the garden from any squirrels. She came bounding in, immediately jumping up at Darek and giving him a slobbery lick across the cheek in the hope he'd repay her by giving up his cookie.

"Sorry, Mr. Vermore!" Alexis gasped, pulling Kimmy down. "No, Kimmy!"

"That's all right," he said, and laughed, breaking off a chunk of his cookie to give Kimmy, who swallowed it whole. "I like dogs. And please, there's no need to call me Mr. Vermore, Alexis. I'm family, remember?"

Alexis nodded vigorously. I've never seen him so engrossed in a conversation with anyone before.

"Although," Darek continued, "I would like to add that in addition to being your family, how about the next few months you also call me your boss?"

Alexis looked completely stunned and glanced at Mum to see if he'd heard correctly. She was beaming at him.

"I would like to invite you to be my intern for the duration of this autumn school term. It won't affect your school hours, but I'd like you to join us in the Vermore London Headquarters on weekends and a few evenings a week. What do you think?"

Alexis just stared at him with his mouth gaping open.

"I know I mentioned to your parents that I'd like to consider you for an internship over Christmas, but it just so happens that I could really do with an extra pair of hands right now," Darek continued, not sure what to do with Alexis's silence so deciding to fill it with more information. "I think it would be mutually beneficial for you to join the team as an intern. We would have the advantage of making use of a terrific brain like yours and you could get some experience of working in a real tech business. Something you might want to consider as a career path someday."

Alexis still didn't say anything. Darek shifted in his seat uncomfortably.

"Of course, if you don't like the idea, please just say. I won't be offended. I know how busy a school term gets and it would be taking on extra work in your free time, so I understand if you want to decline the offer."

"You ... you want ... me ... to be an ... intern?" Alexis eventually managed to whisper.

"Yes," Darek said, furrowing his eyebrows as though he was missing something.

Alexis didn't reply; he stood frozen to the spot. Clara reached over and touched his arm with the back of her hand, before pressing two fingers to his wrist and then examining his face. She took a step back and nodded satisfactorily.

"It's just as I thought," Clara announced to the room. "Cool, clammy skin, rapid pulse and enlarged pupils. Alexis is in shock."

"I see," Mr. Vermore replied, the corners of his mouth twitching into a smile at my little sister's matter-of-fact tone. "And would you diagnose it as good shock or bad shock?"

"Considering all the factors in the situation, including Alexis's hero worship of you, I would conclude it is roughly ninety-two percent of what you term 'good shock,'" she replied thoughtfully, taking a cookie from the tin. "The only negative element contributing to my calculation of eight percent bad shock would be the considerable increase in work outside of school hours."

"Wow," Darek said, his eyes moving from Clara to my dad, who looked so proud he might burst. "This one's a chip off the old block, eh, Professor Beam?"

"Oh, Clara's in a whole different league than me. Only eight years old and her first paper is going to be published very soon, I'm sure of it. She's going to be the most famous scientist in the world," Dad stated, putting an arm round her. She frowned, embarrassed.

"It is definitely good shock," Alexis blurted, finding his voice again. "I would love to be your intern! Sorry, I just... I'm just taking it all in. I've always dreamed of working at Vermore Enterprises one day."

"Well, it's about time that dream came true." Darek held out his hand to shake Alexis's. "Welcome to the team. Have this weekend and next week to settle back into school, and then let's begin."

Darek paused, turning to Mum. "That is, if you're both happy with my offer?"

"I think it's brilliant." Mum grinned, putting a hand on Alexis's shoulder. "You have to work hard, Alexis, and not get into any trouble."

"*Mum*," Alexis hissed through his teeth, looking mortified.

"We so appreciate you taking Alexis on," Mum continued, ignoring Alexis who looked as though he wanted to sink into the ground. "I know things between my mum and your dad weren't... Well, never mind. I'm just pleased that all of that is behind us and you're part of the family."

"Trust me, hiring Alexis as an intern is the least I could do to make up for my father's actions" – Darek hesitated, clearing his throat and looking embarrassed – "really."

I was suddenly desperate to ask what he meant about his "father's actions." That implied that it had been Nolan who had caused the fight with Nanny Beam before he passed away. But Darek didn't offer any further explanation and, collecting himself, he moved the conversation on quickly before anyone had the chance to linger on it.

"Anyway, I know that Alexis is going to be a brilliant addition to the team. And I'll have to keep my eye on you, Clara," he said with a grin. "If I start now, maybe by the time you leave school I'll have persuaded you to have a career in technology, too."

"I've considered it and weighed up the pros and cons, but it would be interesting to hear from someone experienced in the tech environment," Clara replied, giving Kimmy half of her cookie and patting her on the head. "I look forward to discussing it with you in due course."

"Me too." He laughed, before turning his

attention to me. "And Aurora? Want a job at Vermore Enterprises? It's turning into a family affair!"

"I'm not smart like Clara and Alexis," I admitted. "So I don't think I'd be much help."

"Much help? Aurora," he said, watching me intensely, "you have the Beam family superpowers. Don't ever underestimate what you can do."

I smiled gratefully in reply. He checked his watch and stood up, prompting his security men to rise as one, ready to leave.

"I have to get to a meeting, but it's been a pleasure seeing you all. Thank you very much for the tea and cookies and Alexis, I'll see you next Saturday, nine a.m. sharp."

"Yes, sir," Alexis replied.

"Darek, call me Darek," he insisted, waving back at us as he and his security team made their way out of the kitchen and down the hall.

"Goodbye, Beams!"

The front door shut behind him and there was a moment of complete silence until we all burst out cheering, congratulating Alexis on his new internship.

"I can't believe it!" he said, grinning from ear to ear. "I get to work for Vermore Enterprises!"

"This calls for a celebration," Mum announced. "I think ice cream before dinner is in order."

"I should say so," Dad agreed. "Clara, how about you grab the bowls."

While everyone bustled about excitedly, I was able to speak to Alexis quietly in the corner of the room.

"This is great news," I said as he typed at warp speed on his phone, probably telling all his online friends what had happened.

"It's the *best* news," he said, concentrating on the screen. "I wish I could start this second."

"And you'll have the inside track on things."

He looked up. "What do you mean?"

"Vermore Enterprises is playing a key role in finding the Light of the World. You'll know everything that's going on."

"I don't think so, Aurora. I doubt they're going to tell an intern anything important."

"They don't need to tell you anything. You're an expert at getting information from computer systems. You can just fill me in when Mum doesn't."

Alexis gave me a mischievous smile. "As proud as I am right now that you're thinking so rebelliously, I won't be doing anything that puts this internship at risk. For once, I plan on doing exactly what I'm told to do and playing by the rules. Plus, this is *Vermore Enterprises*, Aurora. Not just any company; the biggest and most advanced tech company in the world. If they want to keep things secret, they'll do just that."

"Yes, but I think I could do something to help if I just knew what –"

"Aurora," he gave me a stern look that he must have learned from Mum, "don't try and pry any information from me. You promised Mum and Dad, remember? Nanny Beam, Mr. Vermore and Mum have everything under control and there's really nothing you can do. So just come and enjoy some ice cream."

He put his arm round me and led me to the table as Dad happily put bowls of ice cream covered in chocolate sauce and sprinkles in front of us.

*

That night as I got ready for bed, I couldn't get what he said out of my head and one phrase seemed to be on repeat in my brain.

There's really nothing you can do.

Tidying my room by throwing all the clothes on the bed into a jumbled pile on the floor, I picked up

the special Lightning Girl jacket that Georgie had
designed for me earlier in the year for my countless
photo shoots. I traced the big lightning bolt that
was stitched across the back with my finger and
then let out a long sigh, throwing it across the room
onto the top of the pile.

"Guess I won't be needing that," I said out loud to my empty bedroom.

Because what's the point in having superpowers if you're not allowed to use them?

"Why is it built in the shape of a banana?"

Alexis looked horrified at Mum's question. We were standing on the pavement, staring up at Vermore Enterprises in East London's Tech City area. Alexis had finished his first week interning and Darek had invited us to come along as his special guests and have a tour of the famous headquarters.

"Vermore Enterprises is NOT built in the shape of a banana," Alexis hissed, glancing at everyone coming in and out through the revolving doors to check that no one had heard.

"No, your mum's right," Dad said, nodding and shielding his eyes from the sunlight as he continued to look up. "It's definitely a banana."

"I see a banana," Clara agreed. "Or perhaps a cookie."

Alexis blinked at her. "A cookie? HOW does this building possibly look to you like a *cookie*?"

"A sort of bitten-into cookie," she explained. "Like you've got a delicious circular cookie and then you've taken a big bite out of it. To leave it . . . crescent shaped."

"Oh, yeah!" I exclaimed, knowing exactly what she meant. "Or I was thinking a boomerang. Does Darek have any links to Australia?"

"*No*! Everyone, listen." Alexis sighed in despair, as we all turned to look at him. "It is built in the shape of a *moon*!"

We looked up at the imposing, modern building towering above us.

"A moon?" Mum said, squinting her eyes.

"Yes. A moon. Like Clara even said, *crescent shaped*," Alexis said, shaking his head as though he was talking to a class of teenagers who were just not getting it. "Not a banana; not a cookie with a bite in it; not a boomerang. A *moon*."

"Oh. Right." Dad nodded slowly. "I can see that. A moon."

"I think it looks more like a banana," Clara announced, causing Alexis to bury his head in his hands. "If you look at the very top of the curve, it seems to straighten out horizontally, like the stalk of a banana."

"No, that's just the roof viewing platform," Alexis explained through gritted teeth. "It had to be straight at the top; otherwise you wouldn't be able to stand on the roof. You'd slide off if it was curved."

Clara looked thoughtful. "Did you know that monkeys eat bananas a different way than us? They ignore the stem and instead start at the other end, which is in fact the top of the banana – the stem is the bottom – and then they pinch it and peel. There is less resistance that way and it's a much more efficient method." She paused and let out a long sigh. "We can learn a lot from monkeys."

"How fascinating," Dad said. "I didn't know that."

"Hello!" Alexis cried, waving his arms frantically at us. "Any chance you can focus on me, please?!"

"Sorry, Alexis, of course," Mum said hurriedly, instructing Clara to put her phone away. "We're so excited to be visiting you here at your internship! And the building really is *very* impressive architecturally. I've never seen anything like it."

"Me neither," Clara said, adding, "although in South Africa, apparently there's a building shaped like a pineapple."

"This building is a MOON. A crescent-shaped moon," Alexis seethed, running a hand through his hair. "Mr. Vermore and his architect designed the Vermore Enterprises Headquarters to be in the shape of a crescent moon for a reason. It's symbolic for ambition and pioneering technology; to keep reaching for the stars, like astronauts kept working toward the first moon landing."

"Of course," Dad said, shooting Clara a warning look as she opened her mouth with a quizzical expression on her face. "That makes total sense. It is clearly a moon. And a very impressive moon at that. Shall we go in? I can't wait to see where you work and meet your colleagues!"

Alexis nodded and led the way, already looking exhausted even though it was first thing in the morning. I followed him through

the revolving doors and stepped into reception. I should have expected the interiors of the building to be pretty cool, considering I'd spent a few days over the summer in an underground spaceship-vibe dome that Darek had built for superhero conferences. But stepping into Vermore Enterprises was completely mind-blowing.

The building seemed to go on FOREVER. You'd almost need binoculars to see the other end of it. Everything was glass, from the long reception desk lining one side of the building to the huge spiral staircase slap bang in the middle of the room which led up to the hundreds of floors. The core of the building was completely hollow, with glass offices all around the edges of the walls, and you could see, toward the top, how the staircase curved into the banana shape.

"Whoa," I gasped, much to the satisfaction of Alexis.

"I know, right? Let me get your badges and then we can head down to my floor."

"Down? Don't you mean, up?" Mum asked, pointing at the stairs.

He shook his head. "No, my office is underground. This is only a small section of the Headquarters. There's a load of floors built into the ground as well."

As he left to sign us in at reception, Mum shook her head in disbelief.

"So, this is what my long-lost cousin has been up to all these years," she murmured. "Not bad, is it?"

Dad put an arm around her shoulders. "It's very impressive. But not quite as impressive as being a superhero and a full-time mum."

Mum nestled into his shoulder.

"Or being the best dad in the world who knows everything there is to know about precious stones," she said, looking into his eyes dreamily.

"Bleurgh," I interrupted pointedly, sharing a look with Clara, who was rolling her eyes. "Mum, Dad, we are in *public!*"

Dad laughed and ruffled my hair, which I didn't appreciate because I had spent ages this morning attempting to tame the curls.

I had not been successful.

I'm really glad Mum and Dad are very supportive of each other and everything, even more so considering they had actually separated a while ago. It wasn't easy with Mum being a superhero and being away saving the world all the time. They grew distant. Luckily, once they'd separated, they'd realized quickly that they really loved each other and would do everything to make it work.

But, STILL, that's no excuse for gross, mushy behavior in front of their children.

"All right, let's go," Alexis said, coming over to us with a handful of lanyards and name badges. "I can't wait to show you my office."

"You have your own office?" Dad said, raising his eyebrows.

"Yep." Alexis nodded, puffing his chest out. "I'm the only intern with one."

Alexis led us into the glass elevator, which made my stomach drop as we set off to his floor. On the way he barely stopped for a breath, telling us about the amazing facilities in the building (indoor tennis courts, a spa for lunch breaks, a gaming room, which had video games that hadn't even been released yet) and how cool the people who worked at Vermore were. A lot of them made him a bit starstruck, but there were some other interns who he was getting on with really well.

When the elevator doors opened to his floor, I couldn't believe that we'd gone to the right place. Even though we were underground, it felt as though we could have been on a top floor and for a moment I wondered if Alexis had pressed the right button, but he walked out confidently.

It was so bright, with high ceilings and wide corridors, and it was all glass, with amazing views across the city. Alexis paused halfway through explaining one of Darek's recent inventions when he noticed we'd all stopped to stare out at the London skyline.

"H-how..." I began, too confused to form my question.

"Oh, yeah, it's cool, isn't it? It's just projections," he said, knocking on the glass wall of the corridor. "We're underground, but it's designed to look as real as possible. My office is in here."

He opened the door to his right and we stepped into a spacious room with a very messy desk. Alexis started at seeing someone sitting in his office chair and immediately straightened up, fiddling with the bottom of his shirt.

"Mr. Vermore!" he said, his eyes flickering to the mess across his desk. "I'm so sorry, I didn't know you were here. I was going to tidy but—"

Darek chuckled, standing up to greet us. "My desk is very similar, Alexis. I can never find a thing. They say creativity is a messy business!"

Alexis's shoulders visibly relaxed as he stepped aside to let Mum give Darek a hug.

"I just wanted to pop down to check that you were happy with your tour and to let you all know how well Alexis is doing here," Darek said.

Alexis stared at the floor, shuffling his feet.

"Alexis seems to be loving working for you, Darek," Mum said. "And the building is very impressive. The moon shape is very inspirational."

"Thank you," he replied, "although, sometimes I worry it looks more like a banana."

Clara and I tried to stifle our laughter by having coordinated coughing attacks.

"Shall I get you some water, Aurora?" Darek asked in concern, clapping me on the back.

"I hope Alexis has been working hard!" Dad said hurriedly, keen to change the subject. "If only he was this focused on his schoolwork, right, Kiyana?"

"*Dad*," Alexis hissed.

"He has been a huge help," Darek assured. "He's been assigned a special project. I've just got him on the case, which is why he gets his own office."

"Wow." I smiled at Alexis. "What's the project?"

"It's *top secret*," he replied proudly.

Darek and Mum shared a smile.

"Well, good luck with it, Alexis. And Darek,

it really is very good of you to invite him to intern here," Mum said. "Especially when you and Nanny Beam are so busy with—"

She stopped, glancing at me. She cleared her throat. "Never mind."

"Busy with what?" I asked, jumping on her slipup. "Have there been any updates on the Light of the World?"

"Aurora—" Mum began, but Darek stepped forward to speak.

"Actually, Aurora, there's no reason for you to be kept in the dark. You are Lightning Girl, after all. We're really making progress. I have people in this very building, at this very moment, using the latest facial and vocal recognition technology to track down Mr. Mercury and any accomplice of his. There have been sightings of him in London. We're closing in on him, I'm sure of it."

He bent down slightly to look me right

in the eyes and spoke in a quieter, slightly embarrassed voice.

"Aurora, I let you down at the Superhero Conference. I thought I could protect the Light of the World and I'll never forgive myself for letting Mr. Mercury get away with it." He paused, thinking of the right words. "I know how significant this precious stone is to the world, but more importantly, I know what it means to the Beams. I've waited a long time to have a family. Together, we're going to get the Light of the World back to where it belongs. I won't let everyone down again. I promise."

"Darek," I said, offering him a weak smile, "I know exactly how you feel."

"Oi! Watch where you're shooting those light beams!"

Mr. Crow's furious face popped up from behind the fence as I quickly put my hands behind my back.

"Sorry, Mr. Crow! I was just—"

"That's twice this week my birdhouse has been knocked to the ground," he grumbled, picking up the bright, neon-green birdhouse he'd made himself three years ago.

In those three years, we'd never seen a bird

go near it. Alexis is convinced he saw a sparrow once fly toward it, shriek at the color and fly off again.

"I'm sorry, I'll be more careful."

Our next-door neighbor shook his head. "Honestly, it's not easy living next door to a superhero. Shooting your light beams all over the place, at all times of the day. No wonder I never see any birds in my garden! They're probably scared to death from the array of disco lights!"

"Gerald, what *are* you prattling on about?" Mrs. Crow said, coming out into the garden holding a yoga mat. "How am I supposed to listen to my breath and focus on my center with your whining floating in through the window?"

"It's Lightning Girl," he harrumphed, gesturing over the fence.

"What about her?"

"She's practicing her light beams and she knocked over my birdhouse again."

"Sorry, Mr. and Mrs. Crow," I interjected. "I'll try to be more careful. I was playing with my dog."

I patted Kimmy on the head and she gave a loud bark, confirming my story. I'd discovered a new game which involved shooting light beams in all different directions while Kimmy went bonkers chasing the beams around the garden. She was yet to work out that she couldn't catch light.

Mr. Crow shook his head and muttered something under his breath, while Mrs. Crow watched me suspiciously.

Ever since my and Mum's superpowers had become public knowledge, Mr. and Mrs. Crow had enjoyed giving exclusive interviews to gossip magazines about the trials of living next door to some superheroes. According to these interviews, Mrs. Crow believed we were descended from aliens.

"Playing with your dog, eh?" Mrs. Crow sniffed, peering over the fence to eye up Kimmy.

"Yep," I replied, cheerily. "Watch this."

I closed my eyes and focused on my superpowers. My hands began to tingle and grow warm before they were bathed in a gentle glow and sparks flew from my fingertips. Suddenly, glittering beams of light shot from my palms horizontally and Kimmy barked with joy. She pounced into the air, snapping her jaws at the light and barking until I did it again and again. I laughed, shooting them in all directions across our garden and Kimmy happily snapped away at thin air.

I stopped the display and, ignoring Kimmy's whines to keep going, I turned back to Mrs. Crow.

"Cool, right?"

She was watching me with a disturbed expression on her face. There was a moment's silence before she spoke.

"You're a very … *strange* girl, aren't you?" she said very slowly.

"Um, I guess I'm a little different." I smiled, tracing the swirled scar on my palm. "But maybe you've just seen me in a *bad light.*" I laughed at my joke. "Get it? Bad *light?*"

I wiggled my fingers so that sparks shot from the ends. Mr. and Mrs. Crow did not laugh. I quickly stopped laughing and put my hands behind my back. Kimmy exhaled loudly and lay down with her head on her paws.

It's a real low point when even your dog is embarrassed by your attempts at comedy.

"Never mind," I said hurriedly. "Sorry again for the birdhouse. I promise I'll be more careful."

"I should say so," Mr. Crow said sternly, his

hands on his hips. "Otherwise I'll be making a phone call to the local council."

My phone beeped loudly, and I fumbled for it in my pocket. Mr. and Mrs. Crow didn't take their eyes off me as I read the message.

> Time for a conference call? Got JJ ready and waiting. C xxx

"Ah, I'd love to stay and chat, but I've just got to go and call my friends. Nice to see you, Mr. and Mrs. Crow!" I said chirpily, waving goodbye to them and then tripping over my feet to get back into the house.

I ran upstairs to my bedroom and got my laptop out, quickly opening the call app and then waiting for it to dial. Cherry's face popped up on my screen.

"Hi!" I said, waving at the camera. "I love your hair!"

"Thanks," she laughed, combing her fingers through her newly dyed purple tips. "I took inspiration from Nanny Beam. Hang on, let me get JJ up."

I waited as she typed on her keyboard and suddenly the screen split, and JJ's face loomed into view.

"Hey, team," he said into his camera, leaning back in his chair. "What's been happening?"

I met Cherry and JJ over the summer at the Superhero Conference and even though we'd only spent a few days with each other there, we'd become close friends and they extended

their stay in England so they could come to Nanny Beam's with my family and the Bright Sparks at the end of their trip. Cherry was from Malaysia and JJ was from Nigeria. I felt sad they lived so far away, but we made sure to video call each other at least once a week.

Before the summer, I'd never encountered another superhero, except for my mum. There were quite a few scattered across the world and it was amazing to meet everyone at the Superhero Conference and witness their cool powers. JJ, Cherry and I had been the only children at the conference, and they had helped me to escape when I'd been falsely accused of stealing the Light of the World and locked in a room.

Stuff like that makes you friends for life.

"What time is it where you two are?" I asked. "It's four p.m. here in England."

"It's eleven p.m. here," Cherry said, before

yawning widely. "I've been up reading, hoping I'd catch you after you got home from school."

"Thanks, Cherry," I said. "Next time, I'll make sure it's a normal time for you! What about you, JJ?"

"How many times do I have to tell you, Aurora?" JJ said, raising his eyebrows. "Nigeria and London have no time difference. It's four o'clock here as well."

"Oh yeah! I keep forgetting. It's just weird that you're so far away, but we're in the same time zone. How have you been? How's the soccer going?" I asked, knowing that JJ was still desperate to join the Nigerian soccer team, even though he was only fourteen years old.

"To be honest, I've been concentrating more on karate recently," he admitted. "Nanny Beam was the best teacher and I've been trying to remember everything she taught me in Cornwall."

"Nice." Cherry nodded approvingly. "Have you been getting better?"

"Are you kidding? I'm basically a pro," JJ announced, causing me to burst into giggles as Cherry dramatically rolled her eyes at the screen.

JJ wasn't exactly modest when it came to his abilities.

"The only thing is, I'm not allowed to practice anywhere but outside now," JJ continued. "I was trying out my high kick the other day and I accidentally kicked the wall and knocked the entire thing down. Luckily, it wasn't a wall that was holding up the house or anything, and Mum is now saying she kind of prefers the open space look. And," he added with a grin, "she said it was one less wall to walk through."

Cherry and I laughed. JJ's superpowers were super speed and super strength, like his dad, so it made sense that he'd be able to take down a wall

with one kick. His mum was also a superhero, with the ability to walk through walls.

"How's everything with you, Cherry? Any premonitions?" JJ asked.

Cherry shook her head. "No, none recently. I've been practicing my Sun Gazing, like Nanny Beam taught me, and I definitely feel calmer, but it hasn't brought on any premonitions."

She sighed, fiddling with the headphones that were always around her neck. Cherry had supersonic hearing and the headphones were specially designed just for her and her powers so that she could put them on and then drown out any other sound except the one in the distance that she wanted to hear. It was incredible to see her in action. If she tried, she could hear something as quiet as a candle burning in a house a few doors down.

She also had premonitions. She couldn't control when she'd have them, and she didn't always know what they were about, but she could feel that something big was about to happen. Usually something bad. The night before the Light of the World vanished, she had a dark premonition, but no one would listen.

"How's everything with you, Aurora?" she asked.

I hesitated. "Not great, actually."

"What's wrong?" JJ asked, leaning closer to the screen.

"I can't concentrate on anything at the moment," I complained. "Everyone around me seems to be capable of just getting on with normal everyday life, even though the Light of the World is missing, but I can't focus on anything else. It's too important."

They both nodded in agreement.

"That's understandable. I mean, the Light of the World could be in the hands of the most dangerous person in the world, for all we know," JJ said. "If they destroyed it or something, who knows what could happen to you? Do you think your powers would just . . . explode or something?" His eyes widened. "That would be *so cool*."

"Thanks very much for that super-helpful input, JJ," Cherry frowned. "And anyway, whoever has it clearly doesn't want to destroy it or they would have done that already. Chances are they have other plans for it, whatever those are."

"It's so frustrating sitting here and being expected to do math and history homework when Mr. Mercury is out there somewhere. He's the key to finding the Light of the World, I'm sure of it."

"Yeah, but Nanny Beam and the British Secret Service are on the case, right?" JJ reasoned. "He's got no chance up against them."

"Everyone is involved except me." I leaned back in my chair and sighed. "Even Alexis is allowed to help."

"Alexis?"

"Yeah. You remember I told you he was interning at Vermore Enterprises?"

"Oh, yes!" JJ snorted. "How many times a day does he hear that tagline?"

"Is he enjoying it?" Cherry asked, ignoring JJ.

I nodded. "He's working on a top secret project for Darek and it's taking up all of his time. Since he started interning there, we've hardly seen him. He's very dedicated. And he won't tell me anything about it. I think he's helping MI5 locate Mr. Mercury. It *has* to be something to do with that."

"Not necessarily. Vermore Enterprises develops a lot of technological equipment. I'm sure almost everything they do there is classified, when you think about all their competitors," Cherry pointed out.

"I just feel as though everyone is helping, apart from me." I looked down at my hands. "And I'm supposed to be Lightning Girl."

"You *are* Lightning Girl," Cherry said. "Look, maybe there is something you could do."

"There is?" I asked, looking up.

"Remember in Cornwall, your friend Kizzy

was reading that book about criminals and she read out that passage about the Blackout Burglar? Didn't she say that the lead detective on that case had ended up leaving the police force when no one would believe his suspicions that Mr. Mercury was working for someone higher up?"

I nodded slowly. "Yes, his name was Detective Inspector Bumble. But that was back in the 1980s and he moved to Canada."

"And in Canada they don't have phones?" Cherry said, with a mischievous smile. "Surely you can track him down and give him a call. Ask him what he knows about Mr. Mercury from all those years ago. Maybe you'd get a clue about who he's working with now."

"Cherry," I said, brightening, "you're right! How have I not thought to do this before now? You're a genius! All I have to do is find where this DI Bumble is and get anything I can from him. Thanks, guys!"

"You are very welcome. Even though technically that was Cherry's idea, I believe I inspired her just by being my awesome self." JJ grinned, giving me a thumbs-up.

Cherry shook her head. "Tell me why we stay in contact with him, Aurora?"

"Purely for entertainment value." I smiled, waving at the screen. "I'll let you know how it goes!"

After saying our goodbyes and the screen going blank, I opened my Internet browser feeling a hundred times brighter and more hopeful than I had just moments before. I didn't need to mope around waiting for something to happen any longer.

Finally, I had a new lead.

7

I was *extremely* pleased with myself.

I came down the stairs the next morning feeling very smug because I'd managed to track down DI Bumble's skateboarding business in Canada along with its phone number. It had taken me a LOT of trawling through Facebook and googling the many "Bumbles" out there, but I had finally uncovered THE DI Bumble, the detective who had headed up all of the Blackout Burglar's cases all those years ago.

Even though it was late, I had dialed the

number straightaway and left a voice mail for him asking him to call me back as soon as possible. Vancouver was eight hours behind, so I wasn't surprised he didn't call back last night as it would have been the middle of the day for him. He must have been working and also he might not have wanted to disturb my sleep. But he would be sure to return the call this afternoon when it was his early morning.

I just had to be patient.

"You're in a good mood," Clara commented as I skipped into the kitchen.

She was sitting at the table with several newspapers open in front of her.

I shrugged, crouching down to give Kimmy a big fuss. "It's the weekend. Where's Alexis?"

"At work," Clara replied without looking up. "I don't know whether he's mentioned it to you, but he's got an internship at Vermore Enterprises."

"Yeah. I think he may have mentioned that maybe once . . . or *five hundred* times."

"Did you hear him leave this morning? I heard the front door shutting at about four a.m.," she said breezily, returning to her newspapers.

"What? He left at four a.m.? That's insane! Why did he go so early?"

She shrugged. "He's really dedicated to that new research project of his. He told Mum and Dad he was going to work early, but I don't think they were expecting him to leave *that* early."

"I didn't even know Alexis *functioned* that early," I said, scratching Kimmy's chin, making her tongue loll out the side of her jaw in happiness. "It's pretty impressive how hard he's working."

I stood up and put my hands on my hips as Clara moved to kneel on the chair so that she could lean across the table to reach the newspaper farthest from her and pull it across.

"Clara?"

"Yes?"

"What are you doing?"

"Reading."

"All the newspapers ... at the same time?"

She blinked up at me with her brow furrowed as though *I* was the one being weird.

"It's good to get a wide perspective of opinions on the same news topic," she explained, gesturing to the papers scattered on the table. "That way I can make my own mind up with all the facts and bias laid out in front of me."

I nodded and she returned to her reading.

"Clara?"

She frowned, slowly turning to me. "Yeeeees?"

"When you win the Nobel Prize before even

hitting your teens, will you mention me in your speech?"

She hesitated and then simply said, "I'll see," in a very matter-of-fact tone.

I laughed and turned to put two slices of bread in the toaster.

"Do you know where Mum and Dad are?"

"Out."

"Both of them? Where?"

Clara gave a long, drawn-out sigh.

"Mum is busy saving the world, as per usual. A man in Brighton has built a huge machine in the shape of a crab and is roaming the beaches threatening everyone with its pincers. Mum's gone to sort it out."

"And where's Dad?"

"He's next door, helping Mr. Crow put up his new birdhouse; he said he'll be back in a minute," she said tiredly, gathering together all the newspapers in a pile and hopping off the chair. "I think I'll go and finish my reading upstairs. In *peace*."

I shook my head at her as she left the kitchen and went up the stairs. My sister was eight, going on eighty.

I hummed while I opened the fridge and searched it for the dairy-free spread. I found it at the back on the bottom shelf and grabbed it, shutting the door.

"Hello, Aurora."

I screamed, and the spread flew out of my hand as I jumped about a mile in the air. Aunt Lucinda was standing right behind the fridge door as I closed it, wiggling her fingers at me in greeting.

"What are YOU doing here?" I cried, my heart thudding against my chest from the fright. "You nearly gave me a heart attack!"

She chuckled. "Oh, darling, you know I love to make an entrance."

Aunt Lucinda was Mum's twin sister, but they were total opposites. Mum was calm and sensible, while Aunt Lucinda was completely bonkers and never took anything seriously.

She had powers, too, like all the Beam women, but she was not a fully fledged superhero and certainly didn't want to be one. She preferred to use her powers to get free tickets to the most exclusive VIP events around the world and the best tables in the most upmarket restaurants. She spent all her time on vacation and would spontaneously show up without any warning that she was coming our way.

Aunt Lucinda was great fun (or "irresponsible" as Mum put it), but she also had the extra perk to her powers of being extremely charming and persuasive, something I'd been victim to before, when she'd easily coaxed me into helping her with one of her jewelry-stealing schemes.

In addition to our light-beam superpowers, all the Beam women have an extra ability or quality that they excel in above the ordinary – not an extra superpower, just something we're *really* good at. Mum is very speedy and strong, Aunt Lucinda can charm her way out of anything, and Nanny Beam has a connection with animals that makes them trust her completely.

We were still waiting for my "extra" ability to show itself. It was taking its time.

I picked the spread up from the floor as Aunt Lucinda slid onto a chair at the kitchen table and then we heard a loud *CRASH!* from the hallway.

"What was that?" I asked, stumbling back.

Aunt Lucinda sighed, smoothing out the creases in the trousers of her bright-pink suit. "Just Alfred," she said.

I went to the hallway and saw Alfred, my aunt's ostrich and sidekick, standing proudly in the middle of a pool of water with shattered glass and flowers strewn across the floor.

"He knocked over Mum's flowers and broke the vase!" I pointed out, as Alfred began pecking at the hallway mirror with his sharp beak. "And now he's trying to break the mirror!"

"Yes, I'm afraid he's proving a point," Aunt Lucinda said, rolling her eyes. "He's still very angry at me for lying to him, you see. When I last saw you, Nanny Beam had sent me and Alfred on a little mission abroad for her. Knowing that Alfred hates going anywhere except on vacation, I told a little white lie about our destination and what we were doing there. He still hasn't forgiven me; he was terribly excited about snorkeling in the Great Barrier Reef and now wherever we go he breaks absolutely everything in revenge."

I watched in horror as a large crack appeared across the mirror.

"Alfred! No!" I said firmly.

He stopped pecking at the mirror and craned his neck slowly round so that one beady eye stared at me. He was sporting a very large hat in the shape of a beaver and a hockey sweatshirt with the Canada red maple leaf on the front.

Alfred has always had a very *interesting* taste in fashion, especially for an ostrich.

"That's enough, Alfred," I instructed.

"Mum's going to be very cross."

There was a moment's pause before he turned around to stick out his bottom. Then he proceeded to wiggle his tail feathers defiantly at me before turning back to the mirror and attacking it with twice the aggression he had before.

"There's no use, Aurora," Aunt Lucinda said, amused. "Ostriches are very stubborn. He'll stop breaking things eventually. He just needs to have his little strop."

I winced as the mirror cracked in every which way it possibly could. Alfred stalked proudly over to the stairs and started work on the banister.

"So, darling, how have you been? I hear you had a run-in with the law."

"How do you know about that?" I hissed. "That was supposed to be secret."

"I'm sorry to tell you that your Nanny Beam

knows everything, let me assure you. Imagine being her daughter! Mummy always knew about every time I got into trouble, no matter how well I did at hiding it or pretending it had been Kiyana. She always somehow *knew*. Don't worry, I won't leak a word to the press about your arrest and I have to say, quite frankly, Aurora, I'm more than impressed. I'm very happy to encourage your little rebellious streak."

I jumped at a banging sound coming from the hallway.

"How integral is your banister to the stairs?" Aunt Lucinda grimaced, before brushing her own question off with a flourish of her hand. "I'm sure it will be fine."

"Where did Nanny Beam send you?" I asked, sitting down with her. "Did you find anything?"

"I did. And it would seem you have, too."

I looked at her in confusion. What was she talking about?

"Me?"

"Yes, you." She took a deep breath. "Aurora, why did you contact DI Bumble last night?"

My jaw dropped open. "H... How did you—?"

"DI Bumble called me to let me know he'd received a voice mail from you."

I was so stunned that I didn't know what to say and sat in dazed silence, so Aunt Lucinda continued.

"The mission I was sent on was to go to Canada, track down DI Bumble and get as much information from him as I possibly could about the Blackout Burglar," she explained. "Mummy was well aware that, since moving to Canada to set up his skateboarding business years ago, DI Bumble had refused to speak about his experience with the police force working on the cases involving the Blackout Burglar. He had tried so hard for so long to get someone to listen to him and received nothing but insults, that he felt it better to pretend as though none of it had ever happened."

"You actually went to see him?" I asked in awe.

"Yes. With my knack for charming people into giving more information than they usually would and persuading them round to my way of thinking, naturally Mummy knew I was the best person for the job."

"And what did you find out? What did he tell you about Mr. Mercury? Any clues?"

She raised her eyebrows and leaned back in her chair, picking a bit of fluff off her tailored jacket.

"I was under the impression that after your little arrest, you had promised your parents to stop trying to look for Mr. Mercury. Which was why I was very surprised to hear from DI Bumble that you'd contacted him."

I gulped. "Are you going to tell Mum?"

She threw her head back and let out a high-pitched "HA!"

"Don't be ridiculous, Aurora, what do you take me for? Some kind of snitch? Please," she snorted, as a wave of relief washed over me, "I've broken thousands of promises and most of them to your mum. When we were seven, she made me promise to stop stealing her homework and handing it in as my own, but I continued to do that right up until graduation. Oh, and there was the time when she was learning to drive and she crashed the car into the lake. Mummy was very good about it and Kiyana made me promise not to tell anyone. Of course, thanks to me, it was on the front page of the local newspaper the next day and highly entertaining for everyone in the village."

"So, if you're not going to tell Mum on me, then how come you're here?"

"I came to tell you to stop bothering DI Bumble. He has nothing more to say on the subject and, besides, he absolutely HATES the Beam family."

"Hates us? Why? Surely we're on the same side if he was always trying to arrest Mr. Mercury."

"Oh, it's nothing to do with that," she said breezily. "He hates us because Alfred came along with me, of course, and he was at the peak of his no-snorkeling strop. He snapped every single skateboard in DI Bumble's shop in half, but one. The skateboard he didn't break, he stole and went on to enter and win a very prestigious skateboarding competition, actually. The first ostrich to ever do so," she added proudly.

There was a loud smash from the sitting room.

Aunt Lucinda chuckled. "Ah. Sounds like he's

done with the banister and has moved on to the family photo frames. I had better get him out of here before Kiyana gets back." She checked her watch. "We have a very important brunch to get to with the prime minister. I think Alfred might be in the running for a top job in the Cabinet! He really does have marvelous judgment when it comes to that sort of thing."

"Can't you tell me anything about your mission?" I pleaded as she pushed her chair back and stood up. "What did DI Bumble tell you?"

She looked at me sympathetically. "I'm not keeping anything from you on purpose, Aurora. There are no secrets here. He just didn't tell me anything of interest. Only that he'd always had his suspicions that the Blackout Burglar had been working for someone else."

"Why did he think that?"

"Simply because of a book they found during a raid on Mr. Mercury's flat. The book was apparently about legendary precious stones, including the Light of the World. It was covered with notes, but they weren't in Mr. Mercury's handwriting. From that, DI Bumble assumed Mr. Mercury was being instructed." She put a hand gently on my shoulder. "I'm sorry, Aurora. I didn't get any new leads from him. Now" – she moved to the doorway and called down the hall – "come along, Alfred, we've got to go to your brunch."

There was another loud bang and a crash in response.

"Are you staying in London for a bit?" I asked, following her as she glided down the hallway to the front door.

"Yes. Don't worry, I'll pop in for another visit soon. I hear you're off to Paris on a school trip after break! How marvelous, I just adore Paris. If you want any tips, let me know."

"Thanks."

She swung open the front door and Alfred came stomping through from the sitting room, bustling past me importantly.

"Aunt Lucinda, wait!" I called out, standing in the doorway.

She stopped in the driveway, just short of Nanny Beam's pink flying sports car. She must have let Aunt Lucinda borrow it for her mission to Canada.

"Yes?" Aunt Lucinda said, while Alfred hopped into the front seat and began beeping the horn with his beak impatiently.

"When you said that DI Bumble found a book about legendary precious stones, like the Light of the World, did you mean to say, precious stones . . . *plural?*"

"Of course, I did! There are hundreds of precious stones in the world. Just look at Cartier! Or Tiffany!" she said wistfully. "Just hundreds of them."

Alfred slammed his head against the horn and held it there, so that there was just one long very loud **HONNNNNNNNNNNNNK**. Aunt Lucinda sighed as neighbors began to appear in windows, looking disgruntled.

"Must be off, Aurora. Toodle-loo!"

She slid into the driver's seat and sped off down the road, just as Dad came wandering out of Mr. Crow's house looking very pleased with himself. As soon as he saw me he launched into a speech about how surprisingly good he was at assembling birdhouses. I stood where I was as he strolled back into the house, deep in thought about what Aunt Lucinda had said until Dad appeared again behind me, the color completely drained from his face.

"Aurora," he said cautiously, holding up a bunch of wilted, stomped-on flowers and a photo frame that was completely broken in half, "any chance you can explain what has happened in there?"

We jumped to our feet and burst into applause, our clapping echoing loudly across the empty gym.

Suzie bowed modestly and broke into a wide grin. "So, what do you think?"

She had just finished a practice run of her gymnastics routine and the Bright Sparks had watched in awe at her leaping and dancing to music blaring from the speakers, her gymnastics ribbon swirling in perfect coils over her head.

"Suzie, it was BRILLIANT!" Georgie

exclaimed, giving her a high five. "If you don't win, then there is seriously something wrong with the judging panel. I'm going to make sure your leotard is absolutely perfect, so that it matches your routine!"

"Thanks, Georgie, I can't wait to see it," Suzie said, wiping her forehead before drinking thirstily from her pink water bottle.

"Wow," Kizzy said, shaking her head in disbelief. "You looked amazing. So elegant and graceful ... but at the same time, so strong! How do you do it?"

"How do you not get tangled up in your ribbon?" I asked, causing Suzie to burst out laughing. "If I attempted rhythmic gymnastics, I would definitely just tie myself up in knots. It's seriously cool."

"Thanks, guys." She smiled proudly. "I'm glad you all liked it."

Everyone turned to look at Fred expectantly.

He stood with a pensive expression on his face, rubbing his chin.

"Weeeeeeeell?" Suzie said. "Any comments, Fred?"

He took a deep breath.

"OK, fine. I admit it. That was awesome."

"Yes!" Suzie grinned. "You all witnessed that, right? A compliment from Fred! But there's still so much to work on. The tiniest slipup or mistake could cost me the championship title. I don't think I'll have much free time to work on anything else."

Kizzy grimaced. "I know what you mean; I'm going to be holed up in my room all week

with the homework I've got. There's so much reading to do. I've had to put up an extra bookshelf in my room to fit my books from my extra classes."

"And I'm going to be stuck in the drama department," Georgie said excitedly. "It's so much fun working on these costumes for the school play. And of course, I've got your leotard to finish, which is my main priority," she added quickly, after receiving a stern look from Suzie. "It's going to be *very* sparkly."

"At least you're all doing things you've chosen to do over break," Fred said grumpily.

"Why? What are you doing?" Suzie said.

"I'm grounded."

"For what?"

"I had a little incident. I don't want to talk about it."

We stared at him.

"All right, FINE. I'll tell you," he relented

with a long sigh. "I had a slight issue with some plumbing."

"Plumbing? What were you doing *plumbing*?" Georgie asked curiously.

"I was trying to help, but I made everything worse," he explained with a shrug.

"I know how that feels," I admitted. "At least you didn't end up in prison. What did you do?"

He glanced at us nervously. "Don't. Laugh."

The corner of Suzie's mouth twitched as she attempted to suppress a smile in anticipation.

"I tried to fix the sink and accidentally flooded the house."

"YOU WHAT?" Kizzy cried, as Suzie shrieked with laughter.

"It's not *that* funny," he grumbled, glaring at Suzie and Georgie who were both bent over in fits of giggles. "My mum told me to leave it when the sink was blocked and went off to call the plumber. I thought I'd give it a try myself because I didn't think it would be that hard, but I must have loosened the wrong pipe or something. Anyway, the whole downstairs flooded so I'm not exactly in my family's good books right now." He sighed again. "Especially after my latest report card."

"So, you're grounded for the whole week?" Suzie asked, wiping tears of laughter from her eyes.

He nodded gravely. "But they say to seize every opportunity, so I'll spend the week researching some new pranks to play on *certain* people. By the time break is over, I'll probably be a pro."

Suzie instantly stopped laughing. "I'm warning you, Fred, if you switch my hair spray can for green-hair mist again..."

"One of my more brilliant ideas," he interrupted mischievously.

"It was the day my gymnastics teacher was seeing my routine for the first time!" Suzie snarled. "And I turned up looking like a FROG."

Fred grinned. "More like a goblin in my opinion."

"All right, you two," Kizzy said, holding up her hands as Suzie opened her mouth to argue. "Aurora, what are you up to for break? Are you going to see Nanny Beam in Cornwall?"

"No, she's too busy with ... everything," I said, as everyone's attention turned to me. "I'm going to be spending my break in the library."

"Studying?" Kizzy asked, her face lighting up. "I can join you! We can have STUDY GROUP!"

Suzie rolled her eyes dramatically. "Honestly, no offense, but sometimes I really wonder how it's possible I ended up as part of this nerdy friendship group."

"Actually, I'm not too bothered about homework right now. I wanted to head to the library to research precious stones," I told them.

Kizzy and Georgie shared a glance.

"Like the ones your dad has on display in the Natural History Museum?" Kizzy asked. "Are you helping him out with a new exhibition or something?"

"Ooooooh, is there going to be another exhibition launch party that we can go to? A black-tie one like last time?" Suzie said excitedly, clapping her hands together.

"Because Georgie's mum has just started doing PR for the most *amazing* new dress designer and we could ask her if—"

"It's not for my dad. I'm doing this in secret. And I'm not talking about those kinds of precious stones. I'm talking about *really* rare ones. Precious stones that might not even exist..." I took a deep breath as they looked at me in confusion. "I wanted to talk to you about something Aunt Lucinda mentioned. She said that she went to see DI Bumble in Canada – you remember the detective who'd worked on the Blackout Burglar cases years ago?"

"I remember reading all about him in that excellent criminal history book," Kizzy said. "That was *such* a good summer read. Shame it was only 968 pages long; I feel like there were a lot of historic cases they could have expanded on. And I wish there had been more about the detailed workings of criminal law."

Suzie sighed, lifting her eyes to the ceiling and speaking to no one in particular. "*How* did I end up here?"

"Anyway," I continued, "apparently, in Mr. Mercury's apartment a long time ago, they found a book about legendary precious stones. Like the Light of the World."

"You mean" – Georgie's eyes widened – "there might be others out there with powers?"

I shrugged. "There could be. If there are other stones out there in the world that are just as precious as the Light of the World, then surely this mysterious criminal will be after those too. But" – I hesitated – "I could be completely wrong and when DI Bumble told Aunt Lucinda about the book, he may have meant it was about the kind of precious stones my dad researches."

"It's worth looking into," Kizzy said. "Are you going to talk to Nanny Beam or your mum about it? Maybe they could shed some light if they already know something, or if they haven't thought of that yet, I'm sure they'd be happy to get their teams on it."

"No, I can't tell them. It will only make them cross that I'm still working on finding the Light of the World, and I want to do this myself. Though, do any of you want to help me?" I asked hopefully.

They shared guilty looks and my heart sank, already knowing the answer before they spoke.

"I'll try my best, Aurora, but I've got all this extra homework..." Kizzy said, trailing off.

"And I've got the routine to perfect," Suzie pointed out.

"And I've got to mop the floors at home from now until the end of eternity," Fred said, wrinkling his nose.

"And—" Georgie began.

"You've got the school play's costumes to

sew," I finished for her. "Don't worry, I know you're all super busy. I'll look into it and let you know what I find."

"Aurora, we're never too busy to help you. We're the Bright Sparks," Georgie said. "It's just that, while we have to trawl through library books, Nanny Beam could find whatever information you need at the drop of a hat with her kind of resources. So, it might be best to leave it with them. What can the Bright Sparks do that MI5 can't?"

"Remember what your mum was saying about all of this being dangerous," Kizzy continued gently. "Whoever has the Light of the World is very powerful. It doesn't make sense for you to take this responsibility on while MI5 is working on it."

"I know," I nodded, taking a deep breath and smiling as best I could. "You're probably right. I've got lots of homework to be getting on with, anyway."

"Enough of this work chat," Fred groaned. "It's officially break and we're still standing in the smelly school gym talking about HOMEWORK."

"I don't like to admit it, but Fred's right," Suzie said, flicking her hair behind her shoulder. "Let's get break off to a good start and have an evening of pizza and movies."

"Yes!" Georgie grinned. "Who's hosting?"

Fred glumly raised his hand and pointed at himself. "It has to be me as I literally cannot leave my house."

Kizzy smiled. "Perfect. Thanks, Fred!"

"I'll just call my mum and let her know," he said, getting his phone out of his pocket before looking back at us. "Oh, and you guys might want to bring rain boots for when we get indoors."

9

"What are you doing?"

I snapped my head up and saw Clara standing in my doorway. Her eyes scanned the dozens of open books scattered across my bedroom floor, covered in colorful sticky notes. I was sitting cross-legged in the middle

and, at the moment she'd found me, was resting my head in my hands in despair.

"Nothing!" I replied hurriedly.

She narrowed her eyes at me. "What's wrong?"

"Nothing's wrong. Why would you think something was wrong?"

"Aurora," she said, leaning on the door frame, "you have a sticky note stuck to your forehead."

I lifted my hand and found that she was speaking the truth. I pulled it off and stared at it accusingly.

"How did that get there?"

"You also have one stuck to your knee."

"Look, I'm very busy," I said crossly, crumpling up the sticky notes that had attached themselves to me without me noticing. "Did you want something?"

"I was actually wondering if you knew where Alexis was."

"Mum said he'd gone into Vermore Enterprises today. He wants to spend a lot of break there doing extra work," I explained. "So weird."

"Oh." She glanced at his bedroom door. "He promised he'd let me borrow his new headphones and I'm not allowed in his room without permission."

I laughed. "Yeah, I don't think it would be worth the risk. Last time I went into his room to look for something when he wasn't there, he put my Lightning Girl sneakers in the freezer as punishment. I didn't find them for two days."

She stepped across the bedroom, carefully finding space to tread in between all the books, and hopped up onto my bed, leaning against the wall with her feet dangling over the side. She pulled my duvet over her legs and propped up some pillows behind her.

"Please," I said drily, "make yourself

comfortable. I'm not busy at all."

"Do you think Alexis has been acting strangely recently?" Clara asked, ignoring me.

"I guess. If by 'strange' you mean 'actually bothering to do some work for someone else,' then yes."

"I think he's upset about the internship," she stated.

I stared at her. "Upset? Are you kidding? He's never been happier! Vermore Enterprises is his dream job."

"That's exactly my point. This is his dream situation. But he hasn't been acting happier," she said thoughtfully.

"What do you mean?"

"I think he's struggling with this project Mr. Vermore has given him and he's worrying that he's not achieving the results he should be. Whenever I see him, he seems down and tired." She paused. "Has Mum ever told you what happened between Nanny Beam and Darek's dad?"

"No. Has she told you?"

Clara shook her head. "I don't want to ask, but I get the feeling Darek is really embarrassed about it and wants to make it up to Nanny Beam, even though it was his dad's fault and nothing to do with him. I hope he's keeping Alexis on the team for the right reasons."

"You think he should *fire* him?"

"No! Only, it would be awful if Darek felt so irrationally guilty about whatever it was that his dad said or did to Nanny Beam before he died, that he keeps Alexis in a role that he's too junior for. I don't like Alexis being so down all the time."

"Clara, this is Alexis we're talking about. He always works everything out in the end," I said encouragingly. "It's obvious that Darek loves him and he wouldn't risk giving Alexis anything he can't handle. Alexis will storm this project, just like he wins at everything else, you wait and see."

She nodded slowly. "Anyway, what are you doing with all these books?"

"Homework," I lied.

"You're lying."

"No, I'm not."

"You're a terrible liar."

"I am not a terrible liar!" I protested. "And I'm not lying!"

"You're the worst liar I ever met. Your friend Suzie agrees with me."

"WHAT? When were you talking to *Suzie* about this?"

"Mum thinks so, too. She says it's cute when you lie."

"It is NOT cute when I lie! And I'm not lying!"

"So, you're currently reading books about the Blackout Burglar and other such criminals for … homework?" Clara said, folding her arms and giving me a very stern look. "I can read, you know."

I gulped.

"OK, I'll tell you, but you can't tell anyone," I hissed, standing up to close the door. "Ouch!" I said, hobbling back to the bed. "Pins and needles."

"When you were sitting cross-legged, you were putting pressure on the peroneal nerve behind the knee, which is what supplies the sensation to your lower limbs."

"Thank you, Clara, very helpful."

I slid up onto my bed next to her. "I think there may be more than one precious stone."

"Of course there's more than one precious stone." Clara frowned. "Dad has plenty in the Natural—"

"No, not that kind of precious stone," I corrected. "Precious stones with powers. Like the Light of the World."

Clara's eyes lit up. "You think there are others with supernatural properties?"

"It's a theory. Anyway, I figured that in his old days of thievery as the Blackout Burglar, maybe Mr. Mercury, on instruction from whoever it is he's working for, had gone after other famous stones, which may also have had secret powers. Apparently, DI Bumble found a book about precious stones in Mr. Mercury's old apartment and it was scribbled all over with notes." I gestured to all the books. "I've been reading up to see if there are any famous gems he had his eye on and attempted to steal back then, but so far, none of his crimes really stand out as something that might be linked."

Clara furrowed her eyebrows, something I know she does when she's deep in thought and just about to say something superintelligent.

"I think you're looking in the wrong place."

"What do you mean?"

"You should be looking into books that might refer to precious stones with *powers*. Old legends and folklore books."

I laughed. "You want me to read *fairy tales*?"

"Folklore is one of the most powerful and informative tools available to us," she said sharply, looking at me in such a disapproving manner that I quickly stopped giggling. "How did our family know about the Light of the World in the first place?"

I hesitated before admitting quietly, "From the legend of the Beam ancestry."

"Told to each generation by the generation before. Chances are it's the same for any other such precious stones in existence."

I suddenly felt very silly for making fun of her folklore suggestion and couldn't believe I hadn't thought of it before. I'd been wasting my time reading the same thing about the Blackout Burglar over and over again, and all along my focus should have been on the stones themselves.

"I need to get back to the library," I said determinedly. "Is there a folktales and legends section? Maybe I should research precious stone folklore online, too."

"I have a better idea. You mentioned that there was an annotated book about precious stones in Mr. Mercury's old apartment? Well, Dad has a really good book about the same thing — there's a chance it's a different copy of the same book, or at least similar to the one Mr. Mercury was reading back then."

"Brilliant! Clara, you really are a genius!"

She looked down at her feet modestly.

"Right," I said, reeling with this new wave of hope, "where can I find this book? Will it be somewhere in Mum and Dad's room?"

"Ah, that's the slight catch," she said. "It's not here, he keeps it under lock and key in his office in the Natural History Museum. It's a very old book and the spine is broken because Dad has read through it so many times. According to him, it's one of only a couple in existence."

"Argh!" I slumped onto the bed. "I can't just ask him for it! He'll know it's something to do with the Light of the World and I promised Mum and Dad I'd stop looking into it."

"You could just ask Dad to look through it for you?" Clara suggested. "Maybe Mum and Nanny Beam haven't thought of this theory yet. It might be useful."

I shook my head. "No, I want to do this myself. Otherwise, I'll just be sitting around waiting and I'm bored with being useless."

Clara watched me carefully.

"Well, then, there's only one thing you can

do," she declared.

"What?"

"Steal it."

My jaw dropped open. "WHAT?!"

"Don't look so shocked, Aurora. You're the one who went to prison, not me."

"HOW DO YOU KNOW I WENT TO PRISON?" I cried. "Mum said she wouldn't tell you and Alexis!"

"I have other sources," she informed me breezily. "So does Alexis. We knew before you got home from the police station. Anyway, none of that is important. I think the only answer to you getting your hands on this book without anyone finding out is to *borrow* it from the museum ... without asking." She hesitated. "There. So, it's not technically stealing."

I stared at her in disbelief. "That would not hold up in court."

"What else can you do?"

I thought about my predicament, still a bit dazed at my little bookworm sister suggesting I commit a crime.

"You're right," I said eventually. "I have to somehow steal it from Dad's office."

"*Borrow*," she corrected. "I can help. Not with the breaking into the office bit, but I know where he keeps the book once you get in. It's in the bottom right-hand drawer of his desk."

"Thanks, Clara."

I started laughing.

"What's funny?" she asked, looking up at me all innocently.

"I never thought we'd be sitting on my bed working out how to steal something together," I giggled. "It's a bit weird in terms of sisterly bonding moments."

"Yeah. Although not as weird as finding out

you have the ability to shoot light beams out of your palms. That was an off-the-scale weird bonding moment."

She caught my eye and we smiled.

"OK, so how are you going to break into Dad's office in the museum?" she asked, clapping her hands together. "He's at work all week. It's going to be difficult to get in without anyone seeing you. You might need some help."

"You're absolutely right, Clara," I said, reaching for my phone. "And when it comes to breaking the rules, I know *exactly* who to call."

The following morning, I waited patiently on the pavement a few streets away from my house. A car turned into the road and sped down it, braking hard to come to a halt right in front of me.

The door opened and a long ostrich leg came protruding out.

"Hi, Alfred, how are you doing?"

Alfred got fully out of the bright-pink car, wearing a black turtleneck and a black eye mask. He ignored my question and instead

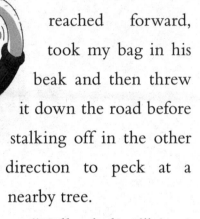

reached forward, took my bag in his beak and then threw it down the road before stalking off in the other direction to peck at a nearby tree.

"Hello, darling!" Aunt Lucinda beamed, getting out of the driver's seat and rearranging her bright-purple sunglasses.

"Hi," I grumbled, going over to pick my bag up from the ground before wiping bits of gravel off it. "Alfred's still in a good mood, I see. Why is he wearing that eye mask?"

"Oh, I told him that you needed a favor and that it was something to do with bending the rules for the greater good, and so he put on his vigilante outfit." She smiled adoringly at him, while bits of bark went flying up in the air. "You know how he likes to dress for an occasion. Of course, it would have been easier to dress for this if we'd actually known what it was we were doing. Your phone call was rather mysterious."

"I can't tell you, Aunt Lucinda. You just have to trust me. It's very kind of you to drive me. Did you collect—"

"I did exactly what you instructed," she interrupted, nodding to the back seat of the car. "See for yourself."

I opened the door and Fred stuck his head out.

"Come on, Lightning Girl, let's get on the road," he said, grinning up at me. "I need to go before my parents notice I sneaked out of the house. We're all ready to go and you're holding us up."

"*We* are ready to go?" I asked curiously. "I don't think so. Alfred is still over there destroying that tree."

"I wasn't talking about Alfred. I was talking about the others."

He gestured behind him, so I leaned forward to look inside the car, furious that Fred had told anyone about our secret mission . . . that is, until I saw who had joined him.

"Aurora, can you *please* tell Fred that he does not need to take up all the space in the car with his *gigantic* elbows?" Suzie huffed, squirming next to him.

"Hey, Aurora!" Georgie waved from the seat next to her. "Plenty of space in the back with Kizzy."

I craned my neck to see Kizzy in the row of seats behind them, lowering her book to check her watch.

"Fred's right, you know. We should get going if everything's going to go to plan," she said matter-of-factly before giving me a little wave. "Hi, Aurora, how are you today?"

"What are you all doing here?" I asked, baffled. "I only told Fred!"

"And he told us," Georgie explained. "You can't go on a Bright Sparks mission without ALL of the Bright Sparks."

"But you're so busy and I didn't want to disturb—"

"Oh please, Aurora, we're never too busy to break into a museum and steal something," Suzie said, looking at me as though I was unhinged. "And did you really think we'd leave you to do something this difficult with only FRED to help? I mean, are you *trying* to get caught? Haven't you had enough of prison?"

"What's that supposed to mean?" Fred grumbled. "I'm the most talented of the bunch. Aurora and I didn't *need* your help."

"Oh, really?" She folded her arms. "Then

why did you call us?"

He shifted uncomfortably in his seat. "I just... I didn't want you to feel left out."

"Sure," she said. "*That's* the reason why."

"You're seriously all coming to help?" I asked brightly, my jaw hurting from grinning so much at how this had turned out. "You are the BEST."

Kizzy smiled warmly. "And we've got a plan, too. Come on, let's get going."

Aunt Lucinda attempted to round Alfred up as I climbed into the car, which I must admit, was a lot more spacious than I remembered. From the outside, it looked like a sleek sports car, but inside it felt like a big truck with a load of gadgets and buttons everywhere. I had asked Aunt Lucinda when Nanny Beam was going to want her car back, but Aunt Lucinda insisted that Nanny Beam was working on a much better model and this was hers to keep.

I don't know how much I believed this story.

Once, Aunt Lucinda told me that a famous Olympian "gave" her the gold medal that was hanging round her neck because they were great friends and he had so many. Then, on the news the next day, that very same athlete made an appeal for the safe return of one of his gold medals after seeing a "bizarrely but unmistakably large bird wearing an Elvis costume" make off with it during his costume birthday party.

To this day, Aunt Lucinda claims it was a big misunderstanding and her returning it to him was a selfless gesture of goodwill on her part.

"Kizzy and Aurora, I can hear you whispering in the back," Aunt Lucinda called out as we drove toward London. "Are you telling Aurora the plan? Why don't you let me in on it? Perhaps I can help."

"Nice try," Georgie said. "Like we already

said, we're not telling you anything about this mission."

"I don't see why not," Aunt Lucinda replied huffily. "Not only am I VERY kindly driving you into London for whatever this nonsense is about, but I also happen to be the world's best at stealthily breaking rules and getting away with it."

"Which is why I knew you were the best person to call to drive us in," I said, studying Kizzy's scribbles and diagrams on the piece of paper she was showing me. "I knew you wouldn't snitch."

"You have my word. But really, darlings, this secrecy isn't necessary! What can possibly be so important in the Natural History Museum? A load of dinosaur bones won't help our plight." She let out a long sigh as no one responded. "And what about my excellent skills in sneaking in and out of heavily barricaded buildings? I have a long list of credentials. I've managed to con my way into some of the highest-profile events in the world. Didn't you see me present that Best Actor Academy Award earlier this year? That wasn't planned, you know. I simply turned up on the day and got in there with just a few distracting light beams and some smooth words."

The rest of the journey into London was spent ignoring Aunt Lucinda as she reeled off her most daring and exciting sneaking-in victories and nodding along to Kizzy's excellent plan at getting into Dad's office without anyone noticing.

When we pulled up to the Natural History Museum, the others swiveled in their seats to face us and Kizzy pointed at her now-crumpled piece of paper.

"Right, first things first," she said in a low voice. "Fred, as soon as you've gotten the key card, you give the signal and we'll set to work. Everyone know what they're doing?"

We all nodded.

"Good. Let's go," she instructed.

"Did I hear someone mention a key card?" Aunt Lucinda said, climbing out of the car and watching us closely.

"Aunt Lucinda," I frowned at her fiercely, "you promised you'd stay out of it. If we get in trouble, I don't want Mum or Dad thinking you helped me. It's better that you don't know what we're doing."

"Very noble," she said, rolling her eyes before getting distracted by Alfred, who had begun to cause chaos by launching into an Irish jig across a crosswalk, making sure the cars couldn't pass through.

"Here goes nothing, Bright Sparks," Kizzy whispered, climbing the steps up to the entrance. "Fred, you're on."

Fred saluted her before disappearing into the crowds of the museum, while the four of us wandered calmly round the room. I stopped and pretended to admire a whale skeleton, suddenly feeling sick with nerves. What if we couldn't pull this off? What if someone caught us and I got all the Bright Sparks into trouble? Mum would ground me FOREVER.

"Everything will be fine," Kizzy said gently, even though I hadn't said a word. "Stop worrying."

"How do you do that? Can you read my mind?" I whispered.

"No. But I am your best friend, so that's kind of the same thing."

After a few minutes, Fred appeared at my side wearing a smug expression. He slipped a key card into my hand.

"Nicely done!" I exclaimed as quietly as possible. "How did you do it?"

He shrugged. "Took it from a security guard in the elevator. The rest is up to you guys."

"Ready, everyone? Let's go," Kizzy said determinedly, leading the way up the steps toward Dad's office.

When we reached the right floor, Kizzy swung into action, seeking out someone who worked at the museum and asking if they could kindly fetch Professor Henry Beam for her, while on the other side of the room the rest of us huddled round a display of what looked like gray pebbles with our backs to her, waiting for the next part of the plan.

"Do you think these are actually important rocks?" Suzie asked, peering through the glass.

"Or do you think someone just picked these up from their driveway and told Professor Beam a bunch of lies?"

"I think that Aurora's dad, with all his many degrees, knows whether they're just rocks from someone's driveway or not," Georgie pointed out.

Out of the corner of my eye, I saw Dad come into the room through one of the "Staff Only" doors. His face lit up when he saw Kizzy.

"Hello, Kizzy!" he said brightly. "What are you doing here?"

"I don't know whether Aurora told you, but I'm taking a lot of new subjects this term and one of them is an extra science module. I thought I'd come here for some research."

"What a brilliant way to spend your break! Research is excellent for relaxation," Dad said enthusiastically, causing Suzie to bury her head in her hands. "How can I help?"

"There's a soil display on the lower floor which I just can't seem to get my head round. Any chance you can spare a few minutes to explain it to me?"

"Kizzy," he said, puffing out his chest proudly. "I couldn't think of anything I'd like to do more. If only Aurora showed this kind of interest in soil! Follow me."

As he marched out of the room toward the stairs, Kizzy glanced back over her shoulder to wink at us before disappearing from view. I nodded to Georgie.

"Go, go, go!"

Georgie gave me a thumbs-up before heading toward the lone security guard, who was yawning at the entrance to the room. Suzie, Fred and I watched as she greeted him and then reached into her bag, pulling out a handful of sparkly sunglasses.

"These are the latest design in security

guard sunglasses," we overheard her telling him as he examined each pair eagerly. "Rumor has it that the head of MI5 has a pair of these ones. Notice the diamanté detail on the rim of the lenses. I actually applied those myself and I think they'd really suit you."

"He's distracted: you're good to go," Fred whispered. "I'll call if your dad comes back; keep your phone on you."

"Gotcha," I said, before Suzie and I sneaked toward the door my dad had emerged from.

I tried not to look at the large "AUTHORIZED ACCESS ONLY" sign as we did a final glance to make sure no one had spotted us, swiping the key card and slipping through the door as the light turned green.

I led Suzie to Dad's office, remembering exactly where it was from the times we'd visited him before. It was in a messy state, with books, files and pens all over the desk. I guess

Alexis was following in Dad's footsteps when it came to office maintenance.

"Where do you think the book is?" Suzie asked, wrinkling her nose at the mess.

"I know exactly where it is," I told her, crouching down at his desk. "Clara told me he keeps it in the bottom drawer."

I pulled at the bottom drawer, but it wouldn't come out. I tried again, rattling the handle.

"It's locked!" I said, my heart sinking. "What are we going to do?"

"Step aside, Lightning Girl," Suzie said in a bored voice.

She whipped a couple of hairpins out from her perfectly sleek ponytail and stretched them out, before slipping them carefully into the lock and twiddling them about. There was a satisfying click and the drawer pulled open to reveal a very large, battered book on precious stones.

"Where did you learn to pick locks?" I asked in awe.

"I guess hanging out with Fred has some advantages," she explained. "The more important question to ask here is, why on earth does your dad bother locking up old books? Is he seriously that much of a nerd?"

I smiled, carefully slipping the book into my bag. "According to Clara, there are only a few of these editions in the world. Mr. Mercury may have had one of them."

We made our way back down the corridor and to the door that led through to the display room. I turned to Suzie.

"You know what to do."

She took a deep breath, composing herself. "Count me in."

"5 – 4 – 3 – 2 – 1."

She slipped through the door, shutting it behind her, and I waited, listening to the

sudden gasps and shouts as chaos began. After a minute I heard a soft tap on the door and I pulled it open to find Fred grinning behind it.

"She's doing a brilliant job," he whispered as I managed to come back through the door without anyone noticing, thanks to Suzie's current display of her gymnastics routine.

The security guard that Georgie had been talking to was now completely distracted by Suzie cartwheeling in very close proximity to the priceless artifacts. While she continued her routine, the rest of us headed out of the room and down the stairs to the exit, Fred texting Kizzy as we went. She soon appeared behind us and we calmly walked out of the museum, waiting for Suzie to join us.

Moments later, she was escorted out by the security guard.

"You really think the routine was that good?" she was saying, as he nodded reluctantly.

"Excellent. You're sure to win the competition. But please don't practice in the museum ever again."

She promised she wouldn't and came over to join us, a smile spreading across her face.

"Bright Sparks, we did it!" She laughed, throwing her arm around Georgie as we all beamed at each other. "Mission complete."

11

"And where exactly have you been?"

I froze in the doorway. Mum was waiting in the hall, her arms folded and her mobile phone clutched in one hand. She did not look happy.

Uh-oh.

"Oh, hey there, Mum!" I squeaked. "I was just at Kizzy's."

"Were you?"

"Yep."

"You were at Kizzy's house down the road."

"Uh-huh! Just like I told you this morning."

"I see. And did you have a nice time at Kizzy's house?"

"Yeah, a great time!" I nodded vigorously. "Kizzy's mum made us some food and we did some homework together and then we watched a movie."

"That sounds lovely."

"It really was."

There was a moment of silence before Mum pursed her lips together.

"The thing is, Aurora, I've just had a nice chat with Kizzy's mum."

A shiver ran down my spine. Oh no. THINK, BRAIN, THINK.

"You . . . you did?"

"Yes, I did," she responded calmly. "And according to her, you weren't at Kizzy's house."

"Oh. . . um. . . well, we were upstairs and she was downstairs, so maybe she didn't realize. . ."

"That's strange. She told me that Kizzy had told *her* she was going to Georgie's house."

"Ah, yes, right, hang on, I've been so silly," I said with a high-pitched nervous laugh. "I meant to say, Georgie's house. Kizzy and I were at Georgie's house. Silly me! Always get those two mixed up. They're so ... well, they have similar ... hair and stuff."

WORK HARDER, BRAIN.

She narrowed her eyes at me as I attempted to swallow the lump in my throat. I could feel the beads of sweat form on my forehead under her glare. Where do parents learn to look at you like this?! They must take some kind of class.

"Interestingly," Mum continued, "after I spoke to her, Kizzy's mum phoned Georgie's parents and then Georgie's parents had to call Suzie's parents because Georgie had said she'd be at Suzie's house."

"Did she?" I croaked. "Right, Suzie's house, oh my goodness, my brain is just going bonkers. Suzie's house is where we were. I don't know why I keep getting so mixed up. Is it hot in this hallway?"

"And then Suzie's parents had to call Fred's parents because Suzie said she'd be at Fred's house," Mum said, ignoring me, her voice getting more and more strained. "And Fred's parents went up to his room, where he was supposed to be grounded, doing his homework, and there was a note on his bed." She paused, staring me down. "Do you know what the note said, Aurora?"

"Ummmm…"

"The note said that Fred had gone to Aurora's house."

I desperately tried to think of something to say as she held up her phone.

"I just got off the phone to Fred's parents. I told them that Fred was, in fact, not here and hadn't been all day. So" – she stepped forward – "do you want to tell me exactly what the Bright Sparks were up to today? Because *clearly* you were up to something, even though you *promised* me that you would stay out of trouble since I picked you up from PRISON just a few weeks ago."

She towered over me as my brain completely shut down, giving me no help at all.

"I... I..."

"Hello, Kiyana!"

A voice rang out behind me and I spun round to see Aunt Lucinda bustling through the front door with Alfred stomping in behind her.

"Lucinda, what are you doing here?" Mum asked, frowning.

"I'm afraid I have come to confess." She sighed, leaning against the door frame so that Alfred could get around her.

Mum and I did the same, flattening ourselves up against the wall as Alfred stalked down the hallway and into the kitchen. A few moments later there was the sound of something being smashed on the floor.

"What exactly are you here to confess, Lucinda?" Mum asked, grimacing as another crash followed. "And make it quick. I don't want my kitchen to be entirely destroyed by your sidekick."

Widening my eyes, I tried to wordlessly beg Aunt Lucinda not to tell Mum anything.

"I acted as the chauffeur today for Aurora and the rest of her school friends," she admitted.

My heart sank. I was busted. Aunt Lucinda

didn't know what we'd been doing at the Natural History Museum, but there was no chance that Mum would believe any story I told her about all of us just fancying a day out there. And as soon as Dad told her that he'd bumped into Kizzy, she would likely guess that had been a distraction technique. I would have to tell her the truth.

"And where did you drive them?" Mum asked, her eyes narrowing.

"Sorry, Aurora," Aunt Lucinda sighed, looking at me earnestly. "I have to tell your mother the truth. It is what family does. I can't break her trust."

I bowed my head, staring at my shoes, and waited for the lecture and punishment to begin. Aunt Lucinda took a deep breath.

"Aurora and some of her friends were helping me to steal back the Dream Diamond," she blurted out.

Mum's jaw dropped to the floor.

"You WHAT?"

"Yes, yes, I know, Kiyana," Aunt Lucinda said breezily, "it's a bad idea to get children involved in stealing a precious jewel."

"YOU THINK?"

"I thought it might be quite a fun mission for Aurora and her friends; you know, something to keep them occupied during their school break."

"You thought *stealing* would be a fun thing to keep them occupied?" Mum cried, looking as though she might explode.

"Now, now, Kiyana, lower your voice. The neighbors will hear! And besides, it's not stealing when the Dream Diamond belongs to me in the first place, as you very well know. It was in our family for years—"

"It never belonged to our family!" Mum interrupted angrily. "Our great-aunt took it from—"

"And then I merely took back what was rightfully mine before you took it from me once again—" Aunt Lucinda continued, ignoring her.

"It was never rightfully yours!"

"I imagine you want it for yourself, as is so often the way with older sisters…"

"HOW DARE YOU! I gave it back to the auction house you stole it from all those years ago!"

"Anyway, let's not hold grudges, darling. I'll forgive you this one," Aunt Lucinda said, waving her hand as Mum's eyes bulged out of her head. "Now, you can't blame darling Aurora for helping her aunt, can you? After all, I didn't tell her what the plan was when we left today. I happily used my power of charm to get her to join me. So that's that."

"Lucinda—" Mum said through gritted teeth, clenching her fists.

"Kiyana, the Bright Sparks failed me. They were unable to find the diamond. You and that dusty auction house have hidden it splendidly. The diamond is safe and sound, and here we are" – she placed her hands on my shoulders – "also safe and sound. No harm done. How about you forgive me, much like I've just forgiven you for robbing me of a priceless heirloom?"

I really felt that Aunt Lucinda might be pushing her luck, but I didn't say anything because in that moment, I couldn't have been more grateful for her and her bonkers cover-up story.

There was a loud crash from the kitchen and Mum buried her head in her hands.

"You look like you could do with a cup of tea, darling," Aunt Lucinda said, tilting her head sympathetically. "Let's go and put the kettle on before Alfred destroys that too."

Mum turned around to head toward the kitchen in a daze, too tired to fight her sister anymore. Aunt Lucinda waited until she was a safe distance away and then leaned in toward me.

"I hope whatever you took today was worth the hours of lectures I'll be receiving from your mum," she whispered into my ear.

I smiled warmly up at her. "It is. I promise. Thanks, Aunt Lucinda."

*

That night, I stayed up late reading through the book using the soft glow of light from my palm. My eyes were getting tired and heavy, and I was sliding farther and farther down into the comfy soft pillows every minute, when I suddenly came upon a passage that made me sit bolt upright.

It was just what I had been looking for.

12

"Wait a minute," JJ said, holding up his hands. "You STOLE from the Natural History Museum?"

I shook my head at the screen.

"No, I didn't steal from the *museum*. I stole from Dad. The book belongs to him. And I'm planning on putting it back, so it's more like borrowing."

"You know what? I can't believe you're doing cool stuff like stealing from museums, while I'm stuck inside writing an essay on the history and structure of glass," he said grumpily.

Cherry made a face into her camera.

"Why are you writing an essay on glass?"

"I was practicing my free kicks and I accidentally kicked the ball with slightly too much super strength." He sighed. "It smashed through a window of the school science building, flew straight through the classroom and smashed right out of the window on the other side."

Cherry's jaw dropped.

"And the teachers STILL haven't caught on that you have superpowers?"

"They think it was a freak accident. Anyway, because I destroyed loads of glass, I now have to write an essay about it."

"That seems a bit unfair," I reasoned. "It was an accident; you didn't mean to break the windows."

"Weeeeeell, that's true, but in defense of my headmaster –" he hesitated – "I was skipping class at the time. I was supposed to be in a science lesson."

Cherry laughed. "Not a very subtle crime then. Aurora, tell us more about this book! It sounds like you went to a lot of trouble to get it. It must be important."

"I wasn't sure whether it was going to be important at all, but then I came across this passage and, well" – I paused, taking a deep breath – "I think I've discovered a potential breakthrough about the Light of the World and its powers. And other precious stones too."

Cherry's eyes widened, and JJ broke into a grin.

"You mean, there really are more precious stones out there with superpowers. COOL!" JJ said, punching the air. "I want one!"

"Keep dreaming, JJ," Cherry said, rolling

her eyes. "What else did it say, Aurora?"

"Hang on," I said, quickly jumping off my bed to shut my bedroom door.

Dad was outside in the garden with Aunt Lucinda and Alfred, but I still didn't want to risk him overhearing my conversation. I was just closing it when Alexis appeared at the top of the stairs.

"Hey." I smiled, waving at him. "You're home!"

"Yep," he nodded, rubbing his eyes, leaning on the banister as he hauled himself up to the top step, "I'm home."

"I thought you were at Vermore Enterprises today. Dad said you left this morning."

"I did, but Mr. Vermore insisted I have the day off."

"Looks to me like you need it. You've been working so hard all break," I pointed out. "Cherry and JJ are on a call if you want to say hi?"

He smiled, following me into my bedroom and waving at the screen.

"Hey, Alexis!" JJ grinned. "How's the internship?"

"It's OK. How are the superpowers?"

"JJ has been using his to destroy school buildings," Cherry informed him, prompting JJ to frown.

"I'm pleased to hear it," Alexis said with a laugh.

"Any secret leads on the whereabouts of Mr. Mercury that you can accidentally let slip?" Cherry asked hopefully, winking at him.

"Sorry, no can do, all top secret stuff," he said, before throwing an arm around me. "But as I've told Aurora maybe six hundred times: don't worry, Mr. Vermore has got the best people in the building working on it and I'm helping out in any way possible. As if I'd ever let anything

happen to my little sister or her superpowers."

I beamed up at him in surprise at such a lovely comment.

"I mean, she may be the biggest, smelliest loser in the world, but that doesn't mean I'm going to let her deal with this on her own."

Ah. Well, it was nice while it lasted.

"I'm going to go take a nap," he said, laughing at my expression and punching me playfully on the arm. "Nice to see you both."

"You're so lucky to have such a cool big brother," Cherry said once Alexis had left and gone to his bedroom. "It looks like the internship is totally wearing him out, though."

"We've hardly seen him since he started," I told them, climbing back onto my bed and balancing the laptop on my knees. "The secret project Darek is making him work on has taken over his life. It's so weird to see him like this. Normally during break, he doesn't emerge from his room until midday and then he just slobs around playing video games and eating everything in the fridge."

"He's dedicated to his art, so nothing else matters," JJ said, in his wisest voice. "I know how he feels."

"Oh, really?" Cherry raised her eyebrows. "I didn't realize that smashing windows was an art."

"That may not be, but soccer is," he said huffily. "I don't understand why I can't just quit school and play for the Nigerian team full time."

"Aurora, PLEASE jump in now and tell us more about these precious stones before we're made to listen to one of JJ's soccer rants again," Cherry pleaded, running a hand through her newly dyed black-and-orange hair.

"With pleasure." I smiled, ignoring JJ blowing a raspberry at us both. "So, get this. According to legend, there are four precious stones with powers."

"Four?" Cherry gasped.

"You're kidding," JJ said.

"Nope, I'm not kidding." I shook my head, reaching for the book and lifting it onto my lap. I held up the page for them to see and they both leaned eagerly toward their screens. "Along with the Light of the World, there are meant to be the following three: the Jewel of Truth and Nobility, the Gem of Wisdom and Peace, and the Heart of Love."

"Whoa." Cherry exhaled. "This is so weird."

"And it's about to get even weirder," I warned her, pointing at the bottom paragraph of the page. "This may just be a strange myth, but it says here that each stone had a guardian to protect it, and a long time ago those guardians believed that there was a possibility they could transfer their powers."

"What?" JJ's forehead crinkled in confusion. "What does that mean?"

"Well, I've read it a few times and it hasn't been expanded on much in the chapter, which makes me think that the author of the book didn't take these claims that seriously," I said thoughtfully. "But according to this one wizard dude from the old days, those people with the powers of the stones, the guardians they call them in here – I guess, like the Beam women, who have the powers of the Light of the World – could transfer their superpowers to others using the stones."

"WHAT?" Cherry almost fell off her chair. "But HOW?"

"Does this mean that, if I wanted, I could transfer my powers to you two?" JJ asked, leaning so close to his camera that I could only see his forehead and eyes. "And I could gain other people's superpowers?"

"I don't think so. I think it's only those whose superpowers are connected to these precious stones."

"Let me get this straight," Cherry began slowly. "There is a possibility that there are four precious stones in the world. So, besides the Beams who have the power of light, there could be potentially three other families who have superpowers from these stones – truth, wisdom and love."

"Yes, that's right," I said. "There *could* be. It is just a legend that's been repeated down the ages, and apart from the details in this book, that legend seems to have almost vanished from history. I've tried searching for more about it online and I haven't found much. I don't think many people believed it, and if they did, they didn't take the time to record anything about it."

"Do you think that's what the bad guy wants with the Light of the World?" JJ asked. "To gain its powers for himself?"

I bit my lip. "Maybe. I don't know. It makes sense, doesn't it? What's the point in having it unless you want its powers?"

"Or you want to sell it," JJ pointed out. "I bet its worth quite a bit."

"Quite a bit? It's *priceless*," I corrected him. "I don't believe they would have gone to as much trouble as they have just to sell it on. Do you?"

"Wait a minute," Cherry said. "You mentioned that the book says it's the guardians who might be able to transfer the powers from the precious stones, right?"

"Right."

"Well, that's great news!"

I looked at her in confusion. "It is?"

"If that's the case, they're not going to get anywhere without the Beams!" she explained excitedly. "They need one of you in order to transfer its powers. The Beam women are the guardians of this stone, surely, considering you have its powers."

"I think so. In the book it seems to talk about just one guardian per stone, but maybe that's changed over the years and there can be whole families acting as guardians, like us. Although, I'm not sure we've done a very good job over the years if we are the Light of the World's guardians." I grimaced. "It was lost for centuries, then discovered a year or so ago and we've already lost it again."

"The point is, if they believe its powers can be transferred, they can't do anything without you or one of the other Beam women. The stone is useless on its own. If this legend is to be believed, then to get its powers, they need one of you," Cherry said, folding her arms triumphantly. "And they clearly don't know that."

"You're right, there's nothing they can do," I said hopefully. "Without the Beams, the Light of the World may be safe after all."

"You just need to find it before they work that out," JJ said.

"Yeah. If this is true, I wonder where the Jewel of Truth and Nobility might be and if the—"

There was a creak outside my door and I instantly stopped talking. My bedroom door was slightly ajar. I hadn't closed it properly. I quickly jumped from the bed.

"Aurora?" I heard Cherry ask from my laptop. "Where did you go?"

I opened my door and saw Alfred standing

at the top of the stairs, pecking at the framed picture of me and Kimmy on the wall. Today, he was dressed in a silver sequined jacket and a top hat that had a matching sparkly brim.

"Hello, darling," Aunt Lucinda said, appearing behind him on the stairs. "We were just coming up to see if you wanted a hot chocolate? Your dad is about to make some."

"No, thanks."

She got to the top of the stairs and, stepping round Alfred, eyed me suspiciously.

"What are you doing so secretly up here? It's a lovely day; your fabulous, obscenely youthful-looking aunt has come to visit you and you are hiding away in your bedroom."

"Just chatting with friends about … homework."

"Uh-huh." She sighed. "Well, I won't bother pressing you. Are you sure you don't want a hot chocolate?"

"I'm sure."

"Come downstairs when you can, darling, Alfred has been performing his cabaret number for myself and your father, and it's really quite the spectacle. Like your dad said, you haven't seen *anything* until you've seen an ostrich tap dance."

She wiggled her fingers at me and swanned back downstairs, Alfred stomping down after her, leaving the now-broken photo frame of me and Kimmy dangling wonkily from one corner.

I'd completely forgotten about Paris.

At school, it was all anyone could talk about. Suzie had even started wearing berets every day in preparation.

"The thing is," she'd announced to us a couple of days before the school trip, "I'm pretty sure it's in my blood."

"What is?" I asked. "Being sporty?"

It was the start of PE and Miss Nimble was leading the stretches. Suzie had been droning on for ages about us forcing her to stand in the back row. Before she was friends with us, she was always in the front row leading the charge in PE, and would often take over from Miss Nimble in barking out instructions.

I'd already zoned out a second or so into her rant.

"No, not being sporty, being *Parisian*," she corrected, adding in random twirls on the spot as she embellished the warm-up stretches. "Keep up with the conversation, Aurora."

"Why? Is someone in your family French?" Kizzy asked curiously.

"No, I don't think so," Suzie replied, bending down to touch her toes. "It's just that I'm so naturally Parisian chic. In both style and attitude."

Fred laughed so hard at her observation that he snorted loudly. Suzie's eyes narrowed to slits as he continued to chuckle while following Miss Nimble's instructions and leaning forward in an attempt to touch his toes.

Suzie gracefully reached toward him and gave him a sharp push.

He toppled forward clumsily, knocking into the student in front of him, who also lost his balance, and they both ended up in a heap of limbs on the floor.

"Everything all right in the back row?" Miss Nimble called out.

"Perfect, Miss Nimble," Suzie smiled sweetly, elegantly leaning forward to touch her toes with ease as Fred scrambled grumpily to his feet.

"That was NOT funny," he hissed.

She grinned. "Personally, I thought it was hilarious."

"I don't think the itinerary is extensive enough," Kizzy quickly interjected, before they could start squabbling. "I've looked through it and there's only half the things I want to see listed."

"We're only there for a few days, Kizzy," Georgie said, as we began the torturous jumping jacks. "The teachers can't fit in everything there is to see in the whole of Paris."

"I don't see why not. If they let me take charge of the schedule, I reckon I could—"

"Ugh, no way," Suzie interrupted. "If they put you in charge, we'd only go to all the boring stuff and miss out on all the cool stuff."

"Like what?" Kizzy retorted. "You think

the *Mona Lisa* by Leonardo da Vinci isn't cool? It's the most famous work of art in the world."

"Yes, and I'm sure that this Leonora di Vicky person is a really great French artist or whatever, but the best thing about going to Paris is the chic atmosphere. I just hope the teachers have put in enough time for us to see some *real* sights. Like that famous hotel, Le Meurice, where all the celebs hang out."

"It's Leonardo da Vinci," Kizzy groaned, her head in her hands. "And he was *Italian*."

"Why is his Mona Whatever in France then?"

"I just want to go to Chanel." Georgie laughed as Kizzy looked pained. "I'm excited about the museums, Kizzy, I promise, but Paris is the fashion capital of the world. One day, I want to live in Paris and learn from the best designers out there."

"I hope you're still going to design Lightning

Girl accessories when you're famous," I said, shooting her a smile.

"How many baguettes do you think I can eat in five minutes?" Fred asked. "Place your bets."

"I think two," Kizzy said.

"I'm betting on a strong three," Georgie declared.

"Two and a half," Suzie said.

"I think two is a push," I admitted. "You have to give him time to chew."

"I reckon I can do five," Fred said, putting his hand on his hips and swirling them in time with everyone else. "Easy."

"That's one a minute!"

"BACK ROW!" Miss Nimble shouted suddenly, making us all jump.

She made her way through the class of swiveling hips to waggle her finger at us.

"You have been talking nonstop! And don't think I didn't see you push into Jeremy, Fred!"

Fred's mouth fell open in protest. "That was Suzie! She pushed me and I accidentally knocked into—"

"I don't want to hear it. You're all being very disruptive. Not like you at all, Suzie. You're usually the star in sports classes," she said, making Suzie blush furiously.

"Sorry, Miss Nimble, we were just talking about Paris. We're very excited."

Miss Nimble's scowl softened. "I see. Well, I am very excited too."

"Are you coming to Paris with us?" Suzie asked hopefully, while Fred muttered something about teachers' pets under his breath.

"Yes, I'm one of the teachers in charge of the trip. And I haven't been able to stop thinking about how wonderful it's going to be." She folded her arms. "But that's no excuse not to pay attention in class, is it?"

She stared us down and we all quickly looked

at the floor, shaking our heads.

"Ten laps. Now!"

"Miss Nimble, please," Fred pleaded as all of us, except for Suzie, groaned. "We promise we'll be quiet."

"Too late, Mr. Pepe. Ten laps and then you can join in with the rest of the class."

"Don't worry, Miss Nimble, we'll be raring to go before you know it. It's an excellent warm-up," Suzie said, clapping her hands. "Come on, Bright Sparks! I'll lead! Let's go!"

She launched into an enthusiastic jog along the side of the gym and we all followed her dismally.

"KNEES UP, BRIGHT SPARKS!" Suzie bellowed, as she stormed ahead. "COME ON, LIGHTNING GIRL, YOU'RE DRAGGING THOSE FEET!"

"What do you think the chances are that we *accidentally* leave her behind in Paris?" Fred said, his mouth twitching into a smile. "Place your bets."

*

When we got home from school, Aunt Lucinda was in the kitchen with Mum. Dad cheerily greeted his sister-in-law before his face fell at the sight of the garden.

"L . . . Lucinda, what's Alfred doing?"

She got up and went to stand next to him to look out.

"He's gardening! What a clever, talented ostrich he is."

"He's tearing apart all my flowers and plants!" Dad cried, rushing out to try and stop him, even though we all knew it was an impossible task to stop Alfred from doing anything.

"It's called PRUNING, Henry!" Aunt Lucinda called after him. "Haven't you ever seen an episode of *Gardeners' World*?"

"How was school, Aurora?" Mum asked as I

gave Kimmy a cuddle.

"Not too bad. Miss Nimble made me do laps. How was your day?"

"Not too bad. I stopped an evil woman from taking over the world using a giant laser beam."

"Equally eventful, then," I said, grinning at her.

"I think I may have developed a new pharmaceutical product in my science class today," Clara said breezily, giving Kimmy a tummy rub. "I need to carry out further tests, but it could be a very important breakthrough in medicine."

"Wow!" Mum smiled, coming over to plant a big kiss on her cheek which Clara immediately wiped off, with a frown. "I can't wait to hear about this. Have you told Dad?"

"She told us all about it on the journey home from school," Alexis informed Mum, reaching into the fridge and pulling out a bottle of juice.

He drank big gulps straight from the bottle, which he knows I hate, but he does it anyway. "It's EXTREMELY interesting."

"And your sarcasm is extremely lacking," Clara retorted, brushing Kimmy's fur off her clothes. "Just because it's nothing to do with computers—"

"All right, boy and girls," Mum said, smiling. "Why don't you go and get changed out of your uniforms and then we can sit down for dinner."

"And I've got a wonderful story to entertain you with while we eat," Aunt Lucinda declared. "It involves your mum being foolish and me saving the day."

"Let me guess," Mum said in a strained tone, putting the oven on. "Is it the one where I got locked in a room during the Superhero Conference, and you and Alfred got us out?"

Aunt Lucinda placed a hand dramatically on her heart and pretended to look shocked.

"Why, Kiyana! Have I told that one already?"

I laughed, following Alexis and Clara upstairs to get changed. When I reached my bedroom, it took me a few minutes to work out that something was different.

I couldn't put my finger on it, but something seemed weird. My eyes darted around the room trying to work out what it was and then it hit me. My desk!

I'd left it . . . *messier* than this.

I scanned the piles of textbooks. I was sure I'd left them strewn across my desk, but they were in an untidy stack now. Almost as if someone had picked them up one by one and piled them up on top of each other as they were looking through them.

And the books next to my bed, too. They had *definitely* been moved.

"Why would someone go through my books?" I said out loud to no one.

A thought crept into my mind. I quickly ran across the room to my bedside table and threw open the bottom drawer.

The book on precious stones was *gone*. My breath caught in my throat.

Don't panic, Aurora, I thought, *don't panic. Maybe you didn't put it back in that drawer when you were last reading it.*

I set to work searching my room, looking in my desk drawers, under the bed, in my closet — it wasn't there. Which means that someone had taken it, and I knew exactly who that was.

I raced downstairs, my heart thudding against my chest in anger.

"Aunt Lucinda!" I said, bursting into the kitchen. "Where is it?"

She looked up from her cup of tea in surprise. She was standing beside Mum and Dad, unable to sit down with their tea because Alfred was lying on his front across the kitchen table, his wings stretched out, loud snores emanating from his beak.

Alfred was partial to spontaneous afternoon naps.

"Where is what, darling?"

"My book!"

"What book?" She looked to Mum and Dad for help but they just shrugged.

"You know what book," I said through gritted teeth.

"I don't know what you're talking about."

She was good. Really good. I couldn't say anything about the book in front of Mum and Dad because that would give everything away. I didn't even know if Dad had noticed it was missing from his office yet.

"You were lurking outside my room the other day when I was talking about the . . . study book. And I know you were interested in that study book. But it's very important that you give it back because I need it for. . ."

I tried to think of a reason.

"Study?" Mum suggested.

"Precisely."

Aunt Lucinda laughed. "I didn't borrow your *study* book, Aurora. What on *earth* would I need a study book for? I wasn't lurking outside your room either, I came up to ask you if you wanted a hot chocolate."

I wasn't fooled. Aunt Lucinda is a very good

actress and I was going to resist any powers of persuasion that came my way.

"Your room is very messy, Aurora," Mum pointed out. "Maybe your book is somewhere under the piles of clothes."

"No, I've checked."

"You want me to have a look with you?" Dad volunteered. "I'm very good at this sort of thing."

"Oh, Henry!" Mum sighed. "You are the *worst* at that sort of thing."

"Aunt Lucinda!" I cried out in frustration. "I know it was you who took my book!"

"I'm afraid you're wrong," she said calmly, taking a sip of tea. "But if I come across this obviously important book, I'll be sure to let you know. What was it about?"

She knew I couldn't say. *She knew.* I pursed my lips and then turned on my heel without another word, storming back upstairs.

"It's funny. When you're that age" — I heard Aunt Lucinda say innocently, as I stomped up each step — "the smallest thing can feel like the end of the world."

"Oh no," Miss Nimble groaned, her eyes wide with fear. "Has anyone seen Fred Pepe?"

I looked over my shoulder down the beautiful cobbled street and when I couldn't see him, turned back and shrugged along with everyone else in our class.

"He'll be around here somewhere, Miss Nimble," Suzie said, adjusting today's bright-blue beret. "Don't worry about him."

"It's not Fred I'm worried about," she replied, putting her hands on her hips. "With him on the loose, it's the city of Paris that has my concern."

We had been in Paris for a few hours and Fred had already managed to: anger the staff in the Eurotunnel when he kept burping louder and louder to test the echo scale of the train; cause chaos at the hotel when we dropped off our bags by attempting to climb out onto the roof in order to get a better view before getting stuck on the fire escape; accidentally hit a stranger, who he thought was Suzie, round the head with a freshly baked baguette; and jumped out at Miss Nimble from behind a big statue, making her scream so loudly that all these French police officers came running over to check that she was all right.

So, it was understandable that Miss Nimble and the other teachers on the trip were worried when he disappeared from sight.

As we waited for Fred to appear, I thought

about how amazing Paris was. Kizzy was right, there was so much to see and do here, but I honestly would have been happy just wandering around the city all day because even the streets seemed beautiful. Off the busy, main tourist areas, there were all these winding paths and cobbled alleyways, lined with loads of colorful buildings, and cute little cafés that had all these wobbly tables and chairs outside.

The thing was, I just couldn't seem to be able to enjoy it properly. I was still filled with worry about the precious-stones book and where it could be. Aunt Lucinda hadn't admitted yet that she'd taken it and it hadn't turned up anywhere at home. The Bright Sparks kept telling me not to stress about it, but it wasn't their superpowers that were in jeopardy.

What if someone really was planning to take the superpowers away from the Beams?

It was weird to think about how not even

a year ago I had no idea that my mum was a superhero or that my family had this centuries-long history of saving the world from bad guys. I had been so terrified of my superpowers and the change they were bringing to my life and my friends, that at one point I'd even decided that I didn't want them anymore.

Now, the idea of my ability to shoot light beams from my hands being taken away made me feel sick. Being Lightning Girl was an important part of my identity these days.

I couldn't concentrate on anything else.

The rest of the Bright Sparks didn't seem to be having that problem. They had thrown themselves into the school trip with every ounce of energy they had. Suzie seemed to have purchased an entire new wardrobe just for the few days that we were here, and Kizzy had been busy informing the whole class about the history of every street we walked down. She had researched it so well that other interested tourists had joined the back of our group when Kizzy had stopped to fill us in about the different buildings we were passing.

Georgie had practically exploded when we'd walked into a square brimming with boutique fashion shops and elegant townhouses. She managed to persuade Miss Nimble to give her five minutes to explore one, before emerging wearing a new pair of sunglasses and a blue-and-gold neck scarf. When I'd asked her how she'd afforded to buy them, she said that the designer had given them to her for free when Georgie had slipped into conversation that she was Lightning Girl's personal stylist.

And Fred... Well, Fred seemed to be on a mission to cause as much trouble abroad as possible.

"There he is!" Suzie cried out, pointing ahead of us.

Fred was sitting in front of a street artist having his caricature done.

Miss Nimble breathed a sigh of relief and then ushered us all to continue following her down the road toward him.

"This bag is so heavy," Kizzy said, stopping to catch her breath and putting her bag on the ground in between her feet. "Let's just have a quick breather. The group will have to wait for Fred before moving on now anyway."

"What have you got in there?" Suzie asked, eyeing up Kizzy's enormous backpack.

"Just a few bits and pieces. My pencil case and stuff."

"What kind of stuff? It looks as though you've got a huge encyclopedia in there or something ridiculous," Georgie laughed.

Kizzy crouched down and unzipped her backpack, revealing its contents: a huge encyclopedia.

Georgie blinked at her. "Oh."

"This is the ultimate encyclopedia on French culture," Kizzy explained, heaving it out, resting it on her knees and flicking through the hundreds of pages. "I thought it might come in handy as a point of reference."

"HELLO. We have phones for that sort of thing now," Suzie said, looking at Kizzy as though she had lost her mind. "We don't need to lug around books with us anymore.

Everything is right here."

She waggled her pink phone in Kizzy's face. Kizzy frowned in response.

"I'm sure the encyclopedia will come in super handy. Phones don't have the kind of information books do," I said, receiving a grateful smile from Kizzy. "Like the precious-stones book, for example."

Suzie rolled her eyes at Georgie.

"You're not still going on about that book, are you?" She sighed. "It's probably just under your bed."

"I checked there and it's not," I told her stubbornly. "Someone took it."

"Maybe it was your dad," Georgie suggested gently. "Maybe he went into your room for something, saw it and thought he'd take it back without getting you into trouble."

"Why wouldn't he just tell me that? No, I think it was Aunt Lucinda."

"But even if it was, is it that big a problem?" Georgie said. "If it's important enough for her to take, then she'll show it to Nanny Beam and your mum, and it will help them find this criminal who has the Light of the World."

"You don't know my aunt like I do," I said. "She doesn't always do things for the greater good, trust me. And she has a thing for precious stones."

"Looks like we're moving," Suzie pointed out, nodding at Miss Nimble who was instructing the group to gather together now that Fred had his caricature neatly tucked under his arm.

Kizzy shoved her encyclopedia back into her backpack and slung it over her shoulders. We caught up with the rest of the class and Fred proudly held up the piece of art for us to admire as we continued down the street.

"Cool, isn't it?"

Suzie wrinkled her nose at the chalk drawing. "It's hardly a da Vicky."

"Da Vinci," Kizzy corrected.

"That's the one," Suzie said.

"I don't ever want to leave Paris," Fred announced cheerily. "It's awesome here, isn't it?"

The others nodded. I was too lost in my thoughts to pay attention and Fred noticed.

"Aurora?" he prompted. "What do you think of Paris?"

"It's wonderful," I agreed hurriedly. "I just wish that—"

"Let me guess," he interrupted, a knowing smile spreading across his face. "You just wish that you didn't have to be in this amazing city with your best friends and the best food in the world because you'd rather be in the library researching jewelry thieves. Am I close?"

"When you put it like that, it sounds awful," I admitted. "But you're pretty much spot-on."

"That's ENOUGH."

Suzie suddenly halted us in our tracks and came

to stand right in front of me with her hands on her hips, her eyebrows furrowed in determination.

"Aurora Beam, I order you to stop worrying about something out of your control."

"But—"

"No buts!" she cried. "Look, you're my friend and I am *not* going to let my friend miss out on this amazing Paris experience. You need to give yourself a break."

"Suzie's right," Georgie agreed. "I haven't seen you relax in . . . forever."

"I'll relax when the Light of the World is back where it should be, just like Darek said," I told them. "But I am sorry for going on about it. I appreciate it must be boring."

"No, it's not boring. We know it's important," Suzie said firmly, flicking her hair back instinctively over her shoulders and then immediately afterward checking that her beret was still perfectly in place. "But we also worry about you. You have a lot on your shoulders, being a world-famous superhero and everything, and I feel that it is our job as your best friends to remind you when it is time to think selfishly for once and *enjoy yourself*."

"Wow," Fred said, looking impressed. "Suzie is actually making a lot of sense. Strange."

"She is!" Kizzy laughed. "And I completely agree with her. Come on, Aurora, why don't you give yourself a day off and enjoy Paris with us? You'll regret it if you don't."

"If you need any more persuading, then I think you should come here," Georgie said.

She had walked a few paces ahead and was standing at the corner of the road, around which the teachers and rest of the class had disappeared. Georgie ushered for us to come and see. We did as she said and took a few steps forward, before turning the corner.

There, looming over us, was the Eiffel Tower.

I've seen it so many times in films and pictures, but that was nothing to seeing it in real life. It was completely breathtaking.

"Whoa," Fred said. "That is one tall tower."

"One thousand and sixty-three feet tall to be exact," Kizzy said, staring up at it.

I was just searching for the words to describe how wonderful it was when a group of teenagers came running toward me in excitement.

"LIGHTNING GIRL! IT'S LIGHTNING GIRL!" one of them shouted at the top of her lungs, causing everyone around us to suddenly turn their heads in our direction.

In just a few moments, we were surrounded by people asking for pictures with me, with the Eiffel Tower in the background, and Miss Nimble came bustling over to make sure I was all right. Georgie, Fred, Suzie and Kizzy jostled with phones that were thrust toward them, attempting to take all the pictures requested.

I posed for all of them, my jaw aching from smiling so much.

"Please can you shoot light beams out of your hands, Lightning Girl?" a little boy asked after he'd had his picture taken with me.

"Uh, I don't think—"

"Pleeeeeeeeease?" he pleaded, his big brown eyes gazing up at me.

"*S'il vous plaît, Fille Foudre!*" a girl on the other side of me added.

I bit my lip and looked to Miss Nimble. "I guess I could. Do you think anyone would mind?"

She grinned. "No, Lightning Girl, if you want to do so, I don't think anyone would mind."

"All right, then," I said, prompting loud cheers and whoops.

Everyone shuffled back to give me a bit of space and Kizzy gave me a thumbs-up, while

Georgie flicked her sunglasses down from the top of her head and over her eyes in preparation.

I held my hands up above my head, pointing my palms toward the sky, and closed my eyes in concentration. Sparks shot from my fingertips and then suddenly bright glittering light beams burst from my palms, sending a controlled wave of energy rippling across my audience, who stood in awe as the beams reached the top of the Eiffel Tower. As I brought my hands down, everyone burst into rapturous applause.

"No matter how many times I see it," Kizzy said, coming to stand next to me, "it never gets old."

"PLEASE can you do that again when we get to the top?" Georgie asked. "It would make the ultimate Snapchat."

"Great idea, Georgie!" Suzie exclaimed. "And I can do a handstand at the top, too. That would look good."

"A handstand at the top! Don't – you're already giving me the heebie-jeebies." Kizzy grimaced, gulping as we made our way toward the elevator. "I've always been a bit funny about heights."

"Don't worry, Kizzy," Fred said. "It's only – what did you say it was? Oh yeah – one thousand and sixty-three feet tall."

The color drained from Kizzy's face and I laughed, linking my arm through hers and excitedly dragging her to one of the most famous sights in the world. Suzie was right. I was finally letting myself have some fun with my best friends, and just had to forget about everything else and be in the moment, otherwise I'd regret it.

We got in the elevator and I traced the swirled scar on my palm with my forefinger before clenching my fist and looking up.

For now, the Light of the World was out of my hands.

Strolling through the entrance of the Louvre Museum the next day, Suzie let out a long sigh and looked as though she was about to burst into tears.

"What's wrong?" Georgie asked. "Did Fred steal your beret again?"

"No, it's safely in my bag. I took it off for the cathedral. Thanks for reminding me." She reached into her bag and pulled her beret out from it. "Notre Dame has made me feel so *sad*. I can't stop thinking about it and it's making me feel blue."

"Really?" Georgie glanced at me. "I thought it was amazing. All that gothic architecture is so intimidating. Kind of scary, in a cool way."

"It was. But while we were in there, Kizzy was telling me all about the book, *The Hunchback of Notre Dame* by Victor Hugo. It's so tragic," she said, her bottom lip wobbling. "Imagine poor Quasimodo locked away up there as a bell ringer. It must have been so *lonely*."

"You do know that didn't actually happen, right?" Fred said impatiently. "It was just a story some dude made up."

"That *dude* saved the cathedral," Suzie snapped. "The cathedral was crumbling and no one was bothering to restore it until he wrote that book. It was so popular that they decided to restore it after all."

"How do you know that?" Georgie asked, looking impressed.

"Kizzy told me all about it. Her encyclopedia

had a whole page dedicated to the Hunchback of Notre Dame and his tragic love story." Suzie sighed dramatically again.

"Speaking of Kizzy," Fred began, seeming keen to change the subject, "where has she gone?"

"She was very excited to get going on checking off the Louvre highlights sheet. I think she's gone ahead," I said, getting out the museum guide and examining it. "We can find her on our way around."

"I think we should start here," Fred said firmly, pointing at the map of the museum first floor.

I looked up at him. "Fred. That's a café."

"Correct," he nodded, before his stomach rumbled loudly right on cue. "I think it's about time for a croissant."

"I think it's *always* time for a croissant in Paris," Georgie said. "Why do they taste a hundred times better here?"

"Before we make our way to the croissants, I think we should go see the *Mona Lisa*," I suggested, pleased to see everyone nodding in agreement. "I have a feeling we might find our missing Spark."

I was right. We made our way to the famous *Mona Lisa* and I wasn't surprised to find a crowd of people gathered round it, holding up their phones and cameras. I was surprised, though, to hear a familiar voice floating through the silence.

Craning over the sea of heads, I saw Kizzy standing as close to the painting as you can get, wearing a Museum Staff badge and looking in her element.

"What is she doing?" Georgie whispered, trying not to giggle.

"I think she may be giving a lecture on the *Mona Lisa*!" I replied, watching her in amazement.

"Now, can anyone tell me the artist of this world-famous oil painting?" Kizzy asked the crowd, as though she did stuff like this every day of her life.

Suzie's hand shot up and she bounced on her tiptoes, wiggling her fingers excitedly.

Kizzy spotted her. "Yes? The young woman in the orange beret?"

"Leonardo da Vicky. OUCH!" Suzie glared at Georgie who had just nudged her sharply in the ribs. "I mean . . . uh . . . da Vinci?"

"Correct!" Kizzy beamed proudly. "Leonardo da Vinci painted this likely between 1503 and 1519, and there are several reasons why it is so famous. Firstly, the techniques used to paint it are quite something, and secondly, the painting is shrouded in mystery. Who is the woman of this masterpiece? Why is she smiling in this manner?"

I scanned the faces of those around me, all completely intrigued and eagerly listening to

Kizzy's talk. I reached for my phone in my bag to take a video of her and noticed I had a notification on my screen.

Missed Call (2)

Alexis

My phone had been on silent all morning

from when we were in Notre Dame Cathedral and I hadn't bothered to check it on the way to the Louvre afterward. Why had Alexis tried calling me *twice*? He never calls me.

I quickly racked my brain, thinking of anything I'd borrowed from him without his permission. I winced as I remembered taking one of his favorite blue hoodies the other day when I was cold and couldn't be bothered to go upstairs to get a sweater. It had been hanging over the side of a chair, so I'd just put that on.

And then spilled a load of Dad's delicious black bean chili all down the front.

And then I'd taken it off and put it back over the chair. Instead of putting it in the wash.

Whoops.

"Aurora, you're missing the talk," Suzie whispered, ushering for me to put my phone away. "She's just wrapping it up now. Anyone got any questions?"

"You know, for someone who claims to be forced to hang out with them, you sure are sounding more and more like a nerd today," Georgie pointed out.

Suzie looked horrified.

"The history of the *Hunchback of Notre Dame*, the fascinating facts behind the *Mona Lisa*." Georgie smiled. "Anyone would think you've been enjoying the culture more than the ... what was it?"

"The chic vibe of Paris that runs through her veins like blood," Fred sniggered.

Suzie whacked him over the head with her Louvre guide to shut him up.

"Whatever," she said, adjusting her beret and sticking her hand high up in the air when Kizzy asked her audience if there were any questions. "Parisians are all about the geek chic."

*

"They offered you a job?"

Kizzy blushed. We were standing outside the Louvre waiting for the rest of the class to gather at the meeting point and Kizzy had just handed back her honorary staff badge and introduced us to the Louvre's Managing Director.

"Not right now, obviously. They just said that if I was interested when I'm old enough, there would be a job for me here."

"That is awesome, Kizzy. Though I'm not surprised, you were great," Fred said, giving her a high five. "What happened? How did you get up there in the first place?"

"I got chatting to someone who was about to start a lecture on the *Mona Lisa* and I think she was impressed by my knowledge. I asked her what it was like to speak about the most famous painting in the world to a bunch of eager tourists and she said, 'How about you find out?'" Kizzy grinned. "Next thing I knew, she'd passed me her badge and I was off!"

"You were a total natural," Suzie informed her. "I now know everything about da Vicky."

"All right people, get together please," I instructed, getting my phone out. "We need a picture of this moment in case one day, Kizzy, you do end up working here."

They struck a pose and I lifted my phone, only to find another missed call from Alexis from ten minutes ago. And a voice mail. Alexis NEVER leaves voice mails.

He must be really mad about the whole black bean chili thing.

"Hang on," I said, going into my call list. "I just need to listen to this."

While the others fell about laughing at Fred pinching Suzie's beret before running about with it, swinging it above his head victoriously with Suzie hot on his heels, I called my voice mail and listened to the message, prepared to get a boring lecture about why it's not OK to borrow my brother's hoodies and not wash them when I spill food on them.

But that's not what it was. Instead, Alexis sounded breathless and panicked. He was talking in such a hushed tone I could barely hear him without really concentrating.

"Aurora, it's me, Alexis. Look, something bad is going to happen. I'm in trouble, I think. A lot of trouble. It's something. . . I think I may have been wrong about something important. I'm in the office and I. . . Just pick up your phone. Aurora, you need to call me back. As soon as you get this, OK? CALL ME BACK."

I had never heard his voice shaking like that before. Something was really wrong.

I called him back and waited as it rang out and went to voice mail. I tried calling again, but the same thing happened. Why would he desperately ask me to call and then not answer?

A text message suddenly flashed up on my

phone from him:

> I need your help, I'm in BIG trouble.
>
> Please come to the HQ straightaway.
>
> Don't tell Mum and Dad!!
>
> Aurora, this is serious, I don't know what to do.
>
> **I need you!!**

I read the message twice to be sure and then without another moment's hesitation, I pelted away from the Louvre and toward the main road.

"Aurora? Aurora, where are you going?" I heard Kizzy's voice ring out behind me.

I desperately looked for a taxi coming from either direction.

"Aurora, what's wrong?" Georgie asked as the Bright Sparks caught up with me and stood around catching their breath. "Are you OK?"

"I have to go back to London. I need a taxi to the Eurotunnel straightaway," I said hurriedly.

"What?" Suzie looked stunned. "Why? What's going on? Has something happened?"

"I don't know," I said, my hands shaking. "It's Alexis. He's left me a voice mail saying he's in trouble and he needs my help. WHERE are all the taxis?! I've seen hundreds when I didn't need one and now there are NONE."

"But we're going back home in a couple of days," Georgie said. "Can't you help him then?"

I shook my head. "No, he texted me too. He needs me at the Vermore office straightaway. Something's wrong, he sounds really panicked. It must be to do with the Light of the World. YES! *Finally*!" I spotted a taxi and stuck my arm out as he put his signal on, turning toward the sidewalk.

"How are you going to get back to London alone?" Kizzy asked with a panicked expression.

"Wait, Aurora, please. We need to speak to Miss Nimble and—"

"I can't wait. You'll have to cover for me. Alexis needs me," I told her, swinging open the car door. "And no matter what, family comes first."

Without waiting for them to reply, I slid into the back seat and slammed the door shut, directing the taxi driver to head to the Eurotunnel as quickly as possible.

The car pulled away and I glanced back at my friends standing frozen on the pavement with stunned expressions, helplessly watching me go.

16

By the time I reached the reception desk at Vermore Enterprises, I practically collapsed onto it. The journey back from Paris to the Vermore Headquarters in London had only taken a few hours in total, but it had felt like a lifetime. I'd tried calling Alexis again but had no luck, so had to make do with texting to let him know I was on my way.

"Alexis ... Beam ... please," I wheezed, having run as fast as possible from the Tube station.

The receptionist looked me up and down in a snooty way.

"Which department?" he said tiredly, as though I was being a great inconvenience.

"I don't know. He's an intern."

He sighed. "There are hundreds of interns here."

"He has his own office downstairs. I can't remember which floor it is, but it's one of the underground ones."

"Very helpful," he said sarcastically, before picking up the receiver. "I suppose I'll just have to try them all until someone has heard of him."

"Thank you," I said, using my sleeve to wipe the sweat from my forehead.

Honestly, I really needed to pay more attention to Miss Nimble when it came to fitness.

I waited while the receptionist dialed each

number, asked if there was an Alexis Beam in the department and then hung up, rolled his eyes and dialed the next one. He glared at me as I continually tapped my fingernails on the desk, but I couldn't help it. I was too nervous. What had Alexis come across in his research? And why was it so bad? It had to be something to do with the Light of the World, otherwise there's no way it would be this urgent.

"Yes, that's right, Alexis Beam. If you could put me through."

I stood bolt upright as the receptionist finally got the right department. He didn't say anything as he waited and then after a few moments, he hung up. I looked at him, baffled.

"He didn't pick up. He must not be at his desk."

"Please can you try again?"

"Look, he's probably popped out and—"

"Please! It's really important!"

"I'm sure it's a matter of life and death," the receptionist said in a bored tone.

"Please, I'm begging you, can you try one more time?"

He looked at me strangely, but then shrugged, picked up the phone again and dialed the number. But Alexis didn't pick up that time either.

"Can you call Mr. Vermore's desk, please?"

"What?" The receptionist spluttered. "You want me to call Mr. Vermore?"

"Yes," I said firmly. "Right now."

"Mr. Vermore is a very busy man, he doesn't have time for—"

"Mr. Vermore is family! He'll have time for

me!" I cried loudly, my voice echoing around the hollow building. "And not only that but also, I am LIGHTNING GIRL and my brother is in trouble and you do *not* want to mess with me right now!"

To give my outburst extra effort, I lifted my hands and made them glow and spark.

The receptionist looked utterly stunned, his eyes as wide as saucers. He scrambled for the phone, dropping it twice as he lifted it to his ear, and gulped loudly as he dialed a number and waited.

"Mr.... V-Vermore, sir, so sorry to b... bother you," he stammered, watching me nervously. "It's just there's a young lady down here at reception asking to see Alexis Beam and he's not picking up his... Yes, yes that's right, Alexis Beam... No, well, he didn't pick up and so I couldn't just let her in and I... Well, yes, I think so... L-Lightning Girl, she says, but I don't... oh... Right, of course, Mr. Vermore... I'm so sorry... No, I didn't... Of course, right away, Mr. Vermore, right away."

He slammed the phone down and stood up, straightening his tie and suit jacket before gesturing toward the elevators. He looked very flushed and as though he might burst into tears.

"Please, Lightning Girl, do come this way. I'm so sorry about the mix-up. I didn't realize who you were at first but do follow me. Let me personally escort you to the elevator."

"Thank you," I said, rushing through the barriers with him. After he pressed the elevator button, I pushed it again and again in the hope that might hurry it up.

The glass doors finally pinged open and I ran in.

"It's floor minus seven, Lightning Girl, to Mr. Alexis Beam's office. Do enjoy your time at Vermore Enterprises," the receptionist called out as the doors closed.

I was so focused on getting to Alexis that this time the elevator didn't make my stomach flip. I felt relieved that Darek knew I was here in case Alexis really was in a lot of trouble. I know Alexis didn't want Mum and Dad to know about any of this, but maybe Darek could help in some way. When the doors opened onto the right floor, I didn't stop to admire the madly realistic projections of the London skyline on the wall. I got to his office and didn't bother knocking, swinging open the door so eagerly, it banged against the wall.

"Alexis?" I called out as I barged in.

The office was empty.

Maybe he'd gone to the bathroom or he had been forced to go to a meeting or something. I'd have to wait here until he got back. Making sure the door was closed, I started poking around his desk in the hope of finding something that might give away why he needed to talk to me so badly. But even though his desk was covered in important-looking files and papers, there was nothing I could see that had any link to the Light of the World or me.

I sat down at his computer and tried to log in to his account. It was password protected and nothing I came up with was right. I put my head in my hands. *THINK, Aurora, THINK! What would Alexis have as his password?*

"Aurora?"

I jumped at Darek's voice and leapt up from Alexis's chair.

"I thought I'd find you in here; the receptionist called and said you were here to see Alexis." He smiled, handing the briefcase he was carrying to one of his ever-present security men. "Are you all right? You look a bit flustered."

"I ran from the Tube," I explained. "Good . . . for my fitness."

"Ah! Good for you," he said. "I'm sorry you had trouble getting in; I've always been a stickler for security. You never know who my competitors might send in to try and crack into my computer system!"

"No problem, I'm just here to see Alexis," I said hurriedly. "I think. . . I think he's in some sort of trouble."

Darek's forehead creased in concern. "What do you mean? What sort of trouble?"

"I don't know," I admitted. "He left me messages and he sounded really panicked. I'm worried about him. He said he thought he might be in BIG trouble and begged me to come here straightaway, but" – I gestured to the empty chair at the desk – "I don't know where he is."

"He doesn't have any meetings today, so he should be here, I know that much," Darek said, before glancing to his security team. "We'll help you look for him."

"I know you're busy. . ." I said apologetically, but he just waved his hand.

"No, not at all. I'll cancel my next appointment; it's not important," he said, typing a message into his phone. "I just hope that. . ."

He trailed off.

"What?" I asked, taking a step forward. "What is it?"

"Well, Alexis has been working on a project for Nanny Beam and myself. A top secret project to . . . locate the Light of the World." He gulped. "He's so good with technology, we hoped that he could help us track Mr. Mercury. Alexis has been very dedicated to the project and . . . I just hope that he hasn't done anything silly."

"You think he may have found out where Mr. Mercury is and . . . gone to confront him on his own?"

"We need to locate Alexis straightaway," Darek said, looking terrified. "You said he told you to come here? That's good, maybe he is waiting for you to join him before he goes looking for whoever it is he's after."

I nodded, feeling sick with nerves. Alexis could be in a lot of danger if he'd tracked down the criminal who had the Light of the World. And I had no doubt that Alexis had succeeded in his task, just like he always does.

"Have you tried the rooftop?" Darek said suddenly.

"The rooftop?"

"Yes, I've come across him several times up there while having my morning coffee. According to the manager of this team, Alexis often likes to go up there to think. Or make phone calls. The reception isn't great down here."

"It's worth a try."

"Let's go," Darek said, taking his briefcase

back from his bodyguard and marching toward the elevator.

"Thank you for helping me," I said as we all huddled into the elevator together and Darek pressed the button.

"No problem," he replied, attempting a weak smile. "I wish Alexis had come to me. I told him not to go after any leads himself. If anything happens to him. . ."

"It won't," I said firmly.

Darek nodded and we stayed silent until the elevator doors pinged open on the top floor.

I followed Darek toward a set of glass steps that led to a door with ROOFTOP TERRACE printed on it in fancy block letters. Darek pushed open the door and held it for me as I hurried through. Although it was a cold day, the skies were blue, and I squinted through the sunshine, too intent on seeing if Alexis was up here to notice the views across London.

The terrace was empty except for one table at the far end. Someone was sitting at it with two men standing on either side of him.

I placed a hand against my forehead to shade my eyes so that I could make out who it was.

Alexis.

His hands were tied behind his back and there was a gag around his mouth. The two men beside him were two more of Darek's security team. I stopped in my tracks and spun round to face Darek, who had been walking behind me.

"What do you think of the view, Aurora?" he asked casually. "You're not too cold, are you?"

"What's going on?"

"Haven't you worked it out yet?" Darek said, a thin smile spreading on his lips.

"W... what?" I stammered, my breath catching in my throat, my heart slamming against my chest.

He smirked triumphantly, as his bodyguards began to slowly surround and close in on me. "Yes, Lightning Girl, I have the Light of the World. I'm the person you've all been searching for."

17

"No," I whispered.

"Oh, yes," Darek sneered, pulling out a chair from one of the rooftop tables and sitting down, resting his hands on his lap. "It's been me all along. I must say, I didn't think it would be so easy to fool the famous Beam women, but I overestimated you."

"What's going on? Let Alexis go!" I cried, balling up my fists in anger as his security team stepped even closer.

I glanced back over my shoulder at Alexis

straining to free himself from the chair, wriggling against the ropes. He tried to say something, but it was just muffled sounds with the gag pulled tightly between his teeth, and even though it was cold on the roof, there were beads of sweat dripping down his forehead.

"No, I don't think I will," Darek replied in a bored voice. "Not until I've got what I want, anyway."

"You're supposed to be our *family*. How could you do this?"

"Family?" He wrinkled his nose in disgust. "Some family you've been to me."

"Nanny Beam trusted you! You're her nephew and my mum's cousin! Nanny Beam loves you!"

"Only once my father was dead," he snapped back. "Didn't she ever tell you the story? Didn't she ever fill you in on why she took me under her wing?"

I didn't say anything. I'd never managed to get to the bottom of what happened to Nanny Beam's brother and it looked like I should have tried harder to uncover the truth.

"No?" He raised his eyebrows. "Perhaps she was in denial. Or maybe she was embarrassed by her brother. Allow me to tell you the story. You see, my father was a brilliant man. As a child he got top grades in everything; he was a child prodigy who grew up to be a highly intelligent and ambitious man, ahead of his time. But no one saw it. None of his family even noticed. His parents barely acknowledged him. Do you know why, Aurora?"

I kept my jaw locked shut.

"You don't even want to guess? It was because of your precious Nanny Beam. His perfect sister," he hissed bitterly. "As they grew up, she was always that bit better than him at everything. And then when she turned fifteen, she showed signs of superpowers, just like her mother. The Beam family trait. Not for the men; only for the women. And her parents were *brimming* with pride. Their darling daughter became quite the superhero. Her powers of light control were more sparkling than her mother's, her intelligence and drive even more impressive. Why would anyone notice a clever brother, when next to him was a superhero sister? It's no wonder he couldn't stand her. He played 'happy families' though, for as long as he could manage. I even remember spending time with my Aunt Patricia as a child. But he couldn't hold in his contempt and eventually they had a big argument. My father stopped talking to his family; he cut off all contact. They barely noticed. Nanny Beam wouldn't even speak about him: that's how little she cared."

"That's not true."

He looked up at me in surprise. "Oh?"

"She wouldn't speak about him *because* she cared," I explained angrily. "Their falling out hurt her more than anything."

"Well, I suppose that's open to interpretation," he said, hardly blinking as he held my eye contact.

"What has all of this got to do with your dad?" I snapped impatiently, gesturing to Alexis.

"It has *everything* to do with my dad," he replied as fury flared in his eyes. "He dedicated the rest of his life to finding superpowers for himself so that he could finally gain the acclaim he deserved! To finally get his revenge on your grandmother!"

I shook my head in disbelief. "*What?*"

"He made it his life's work, proving that the Beam women weren't as special as they thought they were," he spat. "He changed his name to

Vermore and set about finding one of the four ancient stones that he'd come to learn about, to extract their superpowers and return to the Beams more powerful than they ever could be. And he came close, too." He paused, inhaling deeply. "He stole a precious stone from its guardian. The Jewel of Truth and Nobility."

"It exists?" I gasped.

Darek nodded. "Oh, yes, and my brilliant father found it. It was the most beautiful thing he had ever seen. The most beautiful thing *I* had ever seen. He took me to the warehouse where he was working on extracting its powers. He came up with some genius inventions, some magnificent machinery, in his attempts to transfer its powers to him. But he was unsuccessful. He died trying."

Something sparked in my memory.

"The explosion of light in that warehouse," I whispered, recalling the newspaper article I had found in Nanny Beam's house back in the summer.

I'd come across it when I'd accidentally stumbled upon the secret underground spy lair of her house, and at the time I had wondered why she'd have saved a newspaper article from years ago about what seemed to be an unexplained power surge in an empty warehouse.

Darek nodded slowly, his expression darkening. "Yes. The last of his failed attempts."

I didn't say anything as Darek collected himself.

"The precious stone, of course, was unharmed. Nanny Beam collected it from the chaos and returned it to its guardian. Annoyingly, my father didn't tell me from whom he'd stolen the Jewel of Truth and Nobility before he died, otherwise I could have stolen it back rather swiftly. As it was, I had to bide my time in order to finish my father's work. And I decided to be smarter than him in doing so. You know what they say, keep your enemies close." He smirked. "Aunt Patricia tried to contact me after my father's death and I shunned her for as long as I could, broken from losing him and determined to become as successful as possible on my own merits. I didn't need anyone else's help. Then, once I had built a business empire, I reached out to my dear aunt. She came running to my side without hesitation. It's amazing what people will do out of guilt."

"She wanted to help you and you betrayed her," I cried, rage bubbling uncontrollably through me.

"She betrayed my father," he retorted. "She should have paid more attention to him, but instead she enjoyed keeping all the glory for herself."

"Nanny Beam isn't like that!"

"I must say that she is an excellent boss," he said breezily, flicking a bug off his cuff. "Commanding respect from the entire British Secret Service isn't easy, but she has managed it brilliantly. And teaming up with me was a smart move. Together, there really is nothing we can't do. The only thing is, the whole time I've been secretly harboring a desire to find that precious stone again, gain its superpowers and wipe out the Beam family, taking ultimate power over the world."

He cackled loudly like an evil villain in a cartoon.

"Sadly, it wasn't as easy as I thought," he said, sighing heavily once he'd finished laughing. "Your grandmother is a tough nut to crack and as much as she trusted me, I had no luck in getting any information from her about the Jewel of Truth and Nobility. Only she knew its whereabouts. After years of excruciating hard work, becoming hugely successful in the tech world, creating a partnership with superheroes, I began to believe it was all for nothing. And then a miracle happened" – he did jazz hands for effect at this point in his story – "the Light of the World, the most *precious* of the mystic stones, was unearthed and brought right here to London to feature in an exhibition in the Natural History Museum, curated by none other than Professor Henry Beam. BOOM." He clapped his hands together loudly, making me jump. "And do you know what the best part was? *Nobody knew.*"

He leaned forward across the table.

"Not even Nanny Beam," he continued. "No one recognized the Light of the World for what it was, except for me. The perfect swirl on the stone was unmistakable, just as the legend of the four stones had described. It had been so long since the precious stones had been an issue, Nanny Beam was focused on other important things in the world. And there it was, on the front page of the newspaper! Discovered along with a bunch of other stones, and on its way to the city in which I lived and worked." He shook his head at me. "It was fate."

"Not for you," I growled.

"That's not what I believed," he chuckled. "I got in touch with an old friend of mine. I'd worked with the Blackout Burglar in the past, funding his many successful missions, and he was lying low at the time. He was very happy to play the part of a new science teacher at the school the children of the Beam family attended. Once there, all he had to do was to persuade the head teacher to allow a school outing to Professor Beam's *fascinating* new exhibition, gain inside access and scope the place out, ready for the big event. It was all very easy. Of course, there was a slight snag in the plan—"

"The Bright Sparks," I interrupted. "We stopped you."

"Mr. Mercury failed me," he replied breezily. "But I gave him a second chance and he managed to redeem himself."

"The Superhero Conference."

"Brilliant, wasn't it?" He grinned, flashing his perfect white teeth at me. "No suspicion could fall on me because I helped Nanny Beam to protect it. It was *my* security system. The blame falling on you at first was particularly enjoyable for me. And then when David Donnelly was unmasked as Mr. Mercury, no one looked twice at me, the caring Beam family member who had been fooled along with everyone else."

"But I saw you that day. We were together

with Nanny Beam after the helicopter had taken off carrying the Light of the World. How could you be in two places at once?"

"I wasn't." He shrugged, nodding toward the bodyguard standing next to him. "My trusty right-hand man here took off with it in one of my helicopters and delivered it safely to my hideaway in Jamaica until I could return it here to London a few days later, without suspicion, and start working on extracting its powers."

"You sent Nanny Beam on a wild-goose chase," I seethed, narrowing my eyes at him. "Helping her to track someone when it was *you* all along."

Darek smiled happily. "Easy to do when you're the one looking for them. I just made up random information I'd received and off her agents would scamper, always coming back with nothing. It has been a *very* fun game. All the while, I've been working on getting the powers from the Light of the World without interruption. Right under her nose."

"I don't understand."

He frowned. "Which bits don't you understand? Tell me and I'll explain the details to you."

"No," I said, shaking my head. "I understand the details of your story. I just don't understand the reasoning. Why would you go to all this trouble over all these years to betray your family for . . . *superpowers*?"

"Is that some kind of joke?" he asked, looking amused.

"I'm being serious. They're just superpowers. I'd trade my superpowers for my family any day," I said, glancing back at Alexis.

Darek shifted in his chair uncomfortably but then cleared his throat and stood up suddenly.

"Funny you should say that, Aurora. That's exactly why you're here."

He walked around the table to stand directly in front of me.

"I've had the Light of the World in my possession for weeks, but HOW to get its powers? Nothing I tried was working. No machinery, no gadgets, no robot could crack it. I hired Alexis here in desperation. I thought maybe having a Beam under my control might help in some way. I convinced him to work on a special, secret project for me. I told him that Nanny Beam and I had considered the idea of the powers from the stone being transferable. I wanted him to help us to work out how, once we'd found the evil person who had stolen it from us. I told him we'd use it for good. To help the world. And lo and behold, he actually believed me."

Alexis struggled against the rope as Darek spoke.

"He had no idea that I already had the stone. He was a devoted worker and I thought it couldn't hurt to have someone with his brains and determination on the team. I was right. You told him how to do it and he told me."

"I don't know how to transfer its powers," I argued.

"Yes, you do," Darek said. "You found all the information in that book. You just didn't translate it properly. Alexis overheard you telling your little superhero friends and he stole the book and gave it to me."

"The precious-stones book from the Natural History Museum?" I whispered, the truth dawning on me.

"Yes, Alexis took it from your room."

Darek paused and tilted his head at Alexis. "Don't let me forget to give you a raise. Excellent work."

Alexis glared at him and tried to shout something through the gag. Darek turned back to me.

"All the information we can access online these days, and in the end the answer was in a grubby old book. It's funny, I used to have a book just like it, but the police snatched it up after a raid. I haven't lent Mr. Mercury any of my possessions since. So handy of you to find another copy; it didn't have a huge print run. To think I had the answer right there in that book all those years ago, and I had no idea. And the answer was very simple. My father and I had gone about it all wrong, throwing money at advanced equipment and technology development, when all I needed was ... you. Aurora Beam."

I clenched my jaw.

"So, as it suddenly began to dawn on Alexis that I hadn't been completely truthful with him, I got my trusty security team to step in and make sure he couldn't go leaving you any more voice mails that might give my plans away, hence his current state of affairs," he explained, as Alexis hung his head. "Then all I had to do was send you a few texts from his phone begging you to come here, and here you are. No questions asked."

He grinned.

"You're very predictable, Aurora. Which makes you easily fooled. Anyway, the book says that you need the guardian of the stone to transfer its powers, correct? And once you have the guardian, you need to hold the stone with them underneath the power of natural light and its powers will be transferred from them to you."

He blinked up at the sky.

"A lovely crisp day, isn't it? Cold, a bit blustery but" – he pointed his finger upward – "the sun is shining. And here we are."

I stepped backward away from him, stumbling into the strong arms of one of his security men. I tried to break free, but he had me in a tight lock. Darek watched my effort to wriggle out of his grip with a bemused expression before nodding at another one of his bodyguards. They picked up the briefcase he'd been carrying with him and brought it over.

Darek entered the codes into all the locks and the briefcase popped open. He lifted the lid and there was the Light of the World, sitting in the middle.

As soon as the briefcase opened, I could feel something happening. Just by being in the stone's presence, my powers heightened, and I began to feel the tingling warmth run through my arms out of my control.

"I had the briefcase made in the exact likeness of that clever safe box your parents had put it in at the conference, so that your powers wouldn't be affected around it. I even brought it round to your house the day I asked Alexis to intern for me. The Light of the World was in your house and none of you had any idea. That must be very frustrating to know now."

He rubbed his hands together. "And now for the big event! Finally, it's time."

"How do you know this will work?" I cried out desperately. "You might have the wrong guardian of the stone!"

He shook his head. "No, Aurora. I'm certain I've got the right Beam for the job."

I stared at him. "How do you—"

"Your scar," he said simply, glancing at my hand. "The one on your palm. It's the same swirl as the one on the Light of the World. No one else in your family has that. And you've always wondered what your extra ability is, haven't you, Aurora? Your mum is abnormally fast, your aunt is impossibly charming, your grandmother has a connection with animals that no one else in the world can dream of making. It's not by accident that you are the only one in your family with the same mark as the precious stone from which your superpowers come. You don't have an extra ability, Aurora, because *you don't need one.*"

He took a step closer to me, coiled his fingers around my wrist and lifted my hand up.

The swirled scar on my palm was glowing. And so was the matching pattern on the stone.

"You, Aurora Beam, are the chosen guardian of the Light of the World."

18

Everything became a blur.

I felt dizzy and weak as Darek gripped my wrist so tightly I thought my hand was going to snap off. My brain was still processing everything he'd explained and for some reason, I felt like crying, my eyes prickling with hot tears. It was all too much for me to handle. When I'd first seen Alexis tied up on the roof, I'd felt so angry and courageous, whereas now, I felt like I could crumple at any second.

I couldn't be the guardian of the Light of the World.

Could I?

With his free hand, Darek gestured to the bodyguard to bring the briefcase closer. Another bodyguard came over to help him hold me as I struggled to get away.

"Stop, please don't!" I cried out, desperately trying to pull my arm free as Darek reached for the Light of the World.

Suddenly, the door to the roof swung open with a loud *CLANG*. Darek and his men spun round and as I looked up to see who it was, I felt as though I could breathe again.

An ostrich, wearing a pirate hat with a large purple plume feather sticking out of the top, appeared in the doorway.

"Aurora!" Kizzy shouted, running through the door past Alfred, followed closely by Fred, Georgie, Suzie and Aunt Lucinda.

"It's Darek!" I yelled at the top of my lungs. "He's had the Light of the World all along!"

The man holding me tried clapping my mouth with his hand, but I was so fired up at seeing them, I didn't hesitate to sink my teeth as hard as possible into his finger. He yelped, pulling his hand away in pain.

"Darek's the bad guy!" I shouted, just in case they hadn't heard me the first time.

The Bright Sparks wore expressions of determination as they ran toward us across the roof, and their arrival brought back all the courage I'd momentarily lost. I didn't feel weak or dizzy anymore. Together, there was no way we were going to let Darek Vermore win.

The Bright Sparks made me feel brave again.

As Darek's team were all focused on my friends running toward them, they were distracted from me and from the Light of the World. The man holding the briefcase out for Darek hadn't snapped it shut again and the precious stone was fully out on display, connecting with and strengthening my superpowers. I decided not to fight it.

It took just a moment of concentration for dazzling light beams to explode from my palms, taking everyone on the rooftop by surprise. The man behind me was sent stumbling backward from the energy force, releasing my arms; the other holding the briefcase jumped in horror away from me as the light burst right up at him; and Darek dropped my wrist and cried out as though the light powers flowing through my arms had somehow burned his fingers.

It was the perfect distraction.

Darek quickly grabbed the briefcase that had been dropped and clutched it tightly to him, ducking behind his security men. As the bodyguard next to me struggled to his feet, blinking madly after the sudden burst of light, Kizzy swung her French culture encyclopedia through the air with tremendous force, whacking him over the head and sending him flying. The other bodyguard ran at her furiously and she let out a war cry as she swiftly dodged his outstretched arms. She swung the book at the back of his head as he flew past her, taking him down, too.

"Good hit!" cheered Aunt Lucinda.

"See, Suzie?" Kizzy yelled triumphantly, holding the book at the ready again. "Told you this would come in handy!"

"GET THEM!" Mr. Vermore roared at the rest of his men. "GET THEM! *GET THEM!*"

His security team did as they were told, leaping into action, but the Bright Sparks were ready. One of the men who had been standing guard over Alexis left him and ran full speed in Suzie's direction.

"Suzie, watch out!" Fred cried.

Suzie calmly took her beret off and placed it on the nearest table before taking a deep breath and running straight at the man coming toward her. There was a moment of confusion on the bodyguard's face before Suzie launched herself into the air, screaming "**KIAI!**" at the top of her lungs and performing a perfect flying kick.

Her foot connected with the middle of his chest and he went soaring backward to the ground with a loud **"Ooof!"** as the wind was knocked clean out of him.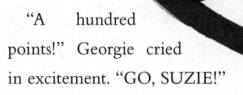

"A hundred points!" Georgie cried in excitement. "GO, SUZIE!"

As Georgie cheered Suzie on, I spotted the other security man who'd been watching over Alexis heading straight for her. I was about to shout in warning, but there was no need.

Pink light beams burst from Aunt Lucinda's outstretched hands, and the sudden wave of their energy forced him to come to a sudden stop, shielding his eyes fearfully from the blinding flash of light.

It gave Georgie enough time to realize what was going on.

She saw him behind her and reached down

to her feet. She pulled off her thick-heeled boot and hurled it at him, hitting him square in the jaw. He held his face in pain before she came at him with her other boot, thumping him in the forehead. As he tumbled to the ground, she whipped out some beautiful, patterned silk scarves from her bag and tied his feet and hands together before he knew what was going on.

"Thank you, Hermès." She grinned, before turning to look up at Aunt Lucinda, gesturing at her boots and scarves. "It's so important to accessorize."

"Totally," Aunt Lucinda replied, pink sparks still flying from her fingers.

I was suddenly grabbed from behind by someone who held me in a tight lock.

"You and your friends won't win this one," Darek growled, as I tried to get out of his grip. He turned to the last security man standing. "STOP THEM!"

Looking a tad nervous considering the fate of his friends, the bodyguard gulped and then lifted his fists and lunged toward Fred. But Fred had been waiting for this moment since the Bright Sparks had burst onto the roof and he wasn't going to let the rest of them have all the fun. He reached into his backpack and pulled out a long string of garlic he must have bought in Paris.

Swinging the string of garlic around his head like a lasso, he narrowed his eyes at the security man, taking aim before launching it into the air. It hurtled at high speed toward the bodyguard, whose eyes widened in panic as the

string of garlic hit him forcefully in the throat, winding itself round his neck and knocking him off balance.

"YES!" Fred exclaimed. "What a strike!"

But the guard hadn't given up. He leapt to his feet, the garlic string dangling around his neck, and darted toward Fred in fury, tackling him to the ground.

"Get. Off. Me!" Fred cried, struggling as the guard pinned his arms down.

Suddenly, the man was struck by a force so strong, it knocked him completely off Fred. He lay in a dazed state. When his vision cleared, he was able to make out an irate pirate ostrich peering down at him.

"Well done, darling!" Aunt Lucinda cheered, clapping loudly. "And do feel free to sit on him for good measure!"

The bodyguard had a split second to yell out in protest before Alfred's big feathered bottom plonked heavily down onto his chest.

"Let her go, Darek!" Kizzy yelled, as they all turned to look at us.

Vermore shook his head, wrenching my arms so tightly behind my back that I yelped.

"You're on your own, now," Suzie said, gesturing to his team scattered about the roof, all of them groaning in pain.

"She's right," Aunt Lucinda told him. "You can't win on your own."

"Yes, I can!" he shouted defiantly.

He reached to the briefcase next to him on the nearest table, punched in the codes and the lid popped open again, revealing the Light of the World.

I felt the tingles rocket through my arms at being so close to the precious stone, and as Darek gripped the Light of the World in his fingers, pulling it out from its setting, I began to panic, which made me lose all control of my powers. Beams of light burst from my palms, but Darek was prepared this time, dodging them and refusing to lose his grip. My beams were joined by Aunt Lucinda's pink ones, which flew toward Darek forcefully, but he squinted through the energy blasts in fierce determination.

This was it. Darek was going to win. He was going to take my powers away from me and transfer them to himself.

"NO!" I heard someone cry as blood rushed through my ears and my vision blurred.

I felt something cold press into my left hand and then Darek's hands closed tightly around mine, holding me up as I let my legs buckle beneath me.

It was over.

I felt as though my heart had stopped.

I wondered what it would feel like to have no superpowers. I wondered what was going to happen now that they had been transferred to someone as unhinged as Darek Vermore. I wondered what he was going to do and how on earth we were going to stop him now. I wondered how I'd explain to Mum how badly I'd let the Beam family down.

And then ... I realized I'd had a LOT of time to be wondering all these things.

Kneeling on the ground, I looked up at Darek towering over me, gripping my left hand. His eyes were filled with panic. I didn't feel different. He didn't look different. Hang on.

Nothing was happening.

He pressed the stone harder into my palm with his hand and blinked up at the sun, waiting for a sign that the powers were transferring through to him.

"NO!" he shouted frantically. "*No!* Why isn't this working?"

"Lightning Girl!" I suddenly heard a familiar voice yell from the other side of the rooftop. "Use your other hand!"

It hit me what they were talking about. Darek was so focused on my left hand, that my right hand had been left free as I'd crumpled to the ground. I lifted my right palm and, holding it right in front of him, I summoned my light beams with all the energy I had left, which wasn't too hard in the end, considering I was literally touching the source of all my powers. A focused stream of light and all the force that came with it blasted out from my hand like a lightning bolt into his face, sending him tumbling backward.

I scrambled to my feet as Nanny Beam appeared at my side.

I grinned, my face buried in her bright-pink hair as she held me tightly to her. "I thought that was your voice."

"Sorry I'm a tad late," she whispered, before pulling back and beaming at me. "Are you all right, Lightning Girl?"

"I am now," I said, watching what seemed like hundreds of agents appear from nowhere and swarm the rooftop with military precision.

Nanny Beam's expression darkened as her eyes moved from me to her nephew.

"Hello, Darek," she said, in a terrifying tone that sent a shiver down my spine.

I would not like to be Darek right now.

The agents surrounding him had picked him up from the ground and were holding him with his hands already tied behind his back.

"I see that I've been grossly wrong about you," she continued.

"Alexis tricked me," he spat in a frenzy. "I had the stone! I had Aurora! I had NATURAL LIGHT! Why didn't it work?"

"Trust me, Darek," Nanny Beam said. "I will make certain that you are the last person in the world to ever know the answer to that question." She nodded at her agents holding him.

"Take him out of my sight."

As they led him off the rooftop, he yelled over his shoulder, "You won't get away with this, Beams! It's not over yet!"

Nanny Beam turned to me and her eyes flickered to my left hand.

"Do you mind?" she said gently, holding out her palm.

"Oh!" I said, suddenly realizing what she meant. I held out the Light of the World for her. I had completely forgotten I was holding it all this time.

She took it from me gently and placed it back in the briefcase before safely shutting the lid.

The tingling feeling in my arms and hands immediately fizzled away and I felt in control again, although I wished I'd held it for that bit longer. It really was the most beautiful thing I'd ever seen. Seeing the Light of the World in all its glory kind of made Dad's obsession with rocks and stones and stuff a little bit more understandable.

A *little* bit.

Before I could say anything else to Nanny Beam, I was suddenly pulled into the tightest hug I had ever found myself in and my face was so firmly nestled into their shoulder, I couldn't even work out who it was until I pulled away and saw Alexis beaming down at me.

"Aurora, you're OK," he said, hugging me again. "I'm so sorry! I messed up everything. It was all my fault."

"You didn't mess up," I said firmly, hugging him back. "He fooled everyone. Are you all right?"

"I'm fine," he said, waving my question away. "I just feel so silly. I can't believe I was the one to give him that book."

"Aurora's right," Nanny Beam said, placing a comforting arm on his shoulder. "He tricked all of us, even MI5." She shook her head. "Even me."

"I'm sorry all the same. I should have checked with you, Nanny Beam, when he first asked me to work on the project." He looked sheepishly at me. "And I shouldn't have stolen the book from your room and given it straight to him. I wanted to impress him so badly, I ended up giving the bad guy the answer to everything."

"To be fair, I stole from my family, too," I admitted in an attempt to make him feel better. "I stole the book from Dad in the first place. So that wasn't a great start."

"And you didn't give the bad guy the answer to *everything*." Nanny Beam grinned, patting the briefcase. "It didn't work. Aurora's still here, powers intact, and the Light of the World is safe again. Darek Vermore will be locked up for the rest of time."

"Yeah," Alexis nodded, his forehead

furrowed in confusion. "I wonder why it didn't work. He followed the book's instructions perfectly. It must all be folktale gibberish after all."

"Folktales are never just gibberish," Nanny Beam corrected sternly before calling over one of her agents. "Now, Alexis, I want you to go with Agent Holden here who is going to take you to the paramedics waiting downstairs to check if you're all right."

"I'm fine," he said, frowning. "Aurora is the one who—"

"Alexis," Nanny Beam said in her sternest grandmother tone. "It's just to be sure. You've been through a lot today. I'll be sending Aurora to the paramedics as well, as soon as I've taken down some more details of what happened here. Now, off you go."

Alexis knew he couldn't argue with her, so he gave me one last hug.

"Aurora, I want you to know that, even after all this, you're still a loser," he said over his shoulder as Agent Holden led him away to the rooftop door. "But an awesome one."

I laughed as I watched him go. "Thanks, Alexis."

The Bright Sparks were huddled together with Aunt Lucinda and Alfred, surrounded by a team of agents, who were running through questions and checking that they were all right.

I was desperate to go over to them, but Nanny Beam held me back a moment longer.

"Before you join your friends, I wanted to apologize myself for putting you in danger. I should have suspected Darek, but I so wanted to believe..."

Her sentence trailed off as she searched for the words.

"That he wasn't like his dad?" I suggested.

She nodded sadly. "It's like you told Alexis, he tricked all of us. This isn't your fault; you couldn't have known. I think what you did for him was amazing. He told me about . . . about your brother and what happened. With the Jewel of Truth and Nobility."

"Did he?" She let out a long sigh. "It was tragic. We got the stone back to its rightful guardian at least, and I'm pleased I never told Darek where it was. So, that's something. There was good in Nolan, I know. He just got" – she shrugged – "lost in it all. Consumed by jealousy. I suppose his son was out for revenge all this time. I really thought I'd gotten through to him."

I took her hand in mine.

"You've got us."

My grandmother smiled. "Yes. Yes, I do. I'm very proud of you, Aurora. Now, I've got to make an important phone call, so you can go on and thank your friends for rescuing you."

"Nanny Beam," I said hurriedly, as she reached for her phone, "can I ask you something?"

"Go on."

"Darek said that I... Well, he thought I might be the chosen guardian of the Light of the World."

"Yes," she said gently, lifting my left hand and admiring the swirled scar. "I think he may be right. It certainly explains a few things, especially why your powers showed themselves so early in your lifetime. The stone knew danger was coming and so a new guardian was chosen. You."

I swallowed the lump in my throat. "But then why didn't it work? The power transfer. If the rest of what that book says about the precious stones is right?"

She looked thoughtful for a moment.

"I'm not entirely sure about any of this, Aurora, but if I had to guess, I'd say that he had the right stone and the right guardian, but the wrong light, perhaps."

"What do you mean? The book said, 'natural light.' That's got to mean sunshine."

"Does it?" She tilted her head at me. "What about the natural light for the stone itself? The Light of the World wasn't found by our ancestor Dawn Beam all those centuries ago in London. It was found—"

"—under the northern lights," I finished, looking up at her in wonder. "The *aurora borealis*."

"Go join your friends," she said, nodding at the Bright Sparks. She pressed one of the options on her speed dial and turned to walk away from me, greeting someone who sounded like an old friend on the phone.

"Oh, I see how it is," Suzie huffed as I pelted toward my friends and the agents stepped aside to let me give them all a big group hug. "Leave us till last. Don't mind us, we just came ALL the way from Paris to be here to save your Lightning butt, only for you to chat with your grandmother for half an hour before saying hello."

"Hello, Suzie." I grinned, throwing my arm around her.

She smiled and patted me on the back. "Whatever. Are you OK?"

"Yes, thanks to all of you. I can't believe you left Paris to come here! What happened?"

"There wasn't any option," Kizzy said firmly. "The Bright Sparks are family and it was like you said when you jumped in that taxi: family comes first. It just took us a few minutes to get another taxi after you zoomed off and then we missed the train you were on and had to wait ages for the next one."

My eyes filled with grateful tears. "I can't believe you did that for me."

"Aunt Lucinda got us here in double time when we reached the UK though," Georgie explained.

"We called her and told her you and Alexis were in a spot of bother. She didn't hesitate to come and get us in the car and fly us to London."

"Although things got a bit hairy when Alfred took the wheel," Kizzy pointed out, giving Aunt Lucinda a stern look.

"Alfred is a splendid driver," Aunt Lucinda retorted indignantly, before adding quietly, "for an ostrich."

Alfred wasn't listening. He was busy trying to steal an expensive-looking watch from the wrist of a secret service agent.

"And the pirate hat?" I asked curiously.

"We were enjoying a luxurious Thames cruise when they called," Aunt Lucinda explained. "You know how he likes to get into character."

"Well, I've never been so happy to see you," I said. "You were all amazing. I can't believe you got up here in time and you took down all of Darek's security team!"

"We'd had some practice, thanks to our Natural History Museum outing," Fred beamed, lifting a Vermore Enterprises key card out of his pocket. "Nabbed this from the guy on reception. Got us through all the doors in this" – he glanced around him – "weird banana-shaped building."

I laughed as Aunt Lucinda smiled warmly at him.

"You took it from the receptionist very smoothly. You have wonderful potential, Fred," she said. "How would you like to learn how to break into vaults? It's about time I imparted some of my wisdom when it comes to bending the rules."

Fred looked thrilled.

"Sorry to interrupt," Nanny Beam said, coming over and holding her phone out, "but my friend would like to have a word with you, Aurora."

I took the phone from her and held it up to my ear, stepping to the side as the others talked among themselves about the events of the day.

"Hello?" I said into the phone, looking at Nanny Beam in confusion. She just smiled knowingly at me.

"Hello, Lightning Girl," said a voice that I recognized straightaway and made me almost drop the phone. "It's the Queen. I hear you've saved the day."

20

"And that was probably the weirdest, most surreal conversation of my life," I admitted, before adding, "except for this one, right now. Obviously."

The Queen chuckled. She had sat patiently, listening to the story from beginning to end, without any interruptions, even though I knew at some points I'd rambled on a bit. She'd been such a good listener and seemed so interested in all the details, I had kind of forgotten that I was in Buckingham Palace talking to the head of the Royal Family.

I wish I hadn't gone on so much about the shape of the Vermore building.

I had actually stood up and arched my body into a curve with my arms outstretched to demonstrate the banana shape. I had acted out being a banana to the QUEEN OF ENGLAND.

That was probably unnecessary.

Still, she hadn't seemed creeped out by that or any of the other parts of the story. She'd nodded and laughed and gasped in all the right places. A butler had now refreshed her teacup four times in the period I'd been speaking.

"It's quite a story," she said, offering me some more tea, which I declined. "I'm glad we got the man in the end. You and your friends were very brave indeed. None of you hesitated to throw yourself into danger to protect each other. And in turn, protect our country from a very dangerous person. That's why I awarded you that medal."

"Thank you, ma'am," I said, bowing my head slightly in what I hoped was a gracious manner because that's what people always do in the movies. "It's weird, though. You don't really think about the danger. You just . . . do it."

She nodded slowly. "I hear you have plans for the Light of the World."

"Yes. I don't think it was lost for centuries before it was discovered; I think it was there for a reason. I want to take it back to where it belongs."

"A new adventure," she remarked, putting down her teacup. "I would have thought you'd want some downtime after such a busy term. You don't want to relax and have some fun over Christmas?"

"It's not that; it's just if I *am* the chosen

guardian, then I have to do the right thing for the precious stone. I mean, I want to go and return it, but even if I didn't... Well" – I hesitated – "I wouldn't really have a choice. It's my duty."

Her sparkling eyes bored into mine. "Yes. If anyone understands that side of things, it's me."

She looked pensive for a moment, so I didn't say anything, waiting for her to speak and listening to the quite comforting ticking sound coming from the old grandfather clock in the corner of the room.

"In return for you telling me your story, I would like to tell you another, if you don't mind. But first, I need my friend to help me explain the finer details."

She nodded to one of the butlers, who bowed his head before opening the door and letting Nanny Beam in. She thanked the security woman who pulled a chair up for her next to mine and flashed a grin in my direction.

The Queen stood up and addressed all the security team and the butlers in the room.

"Thank you. If everyone could now leave us, I would be very grateful," she announced, before turning to Joe, the butler who had welcomed us and was standing by the fireplace. I hadn't noticed that he had been holding a wooden box this whole time.

"And if you could leave that here with me, Joe, thank you."

The servants all bowed their heads before exiting the room swiftly. Joe placed the wooden box very carefully on the table after the tea tray had been removed by another butler, and left the room last, shutting the door carefully behind him.

"Have you had a nice time?" Nanny Beam asked.

"Your delightful granddaughter has been

telling me everything that happened," the Queen informed her, smiling warmly. "She's as brave as you described to me, Patricia, and more."

"She's just like her grandmother. Simply fabulous," Nanny Beam said.

"I'm pleased to see she hasn't gone down the same route in terms of hair color," the Queen commented, with a mischievous glint in her eye.

"Now, now, I thought you said you liked this color!"

"I do! It's just VERY loud, isn't it?" the Queen teased.

"Oh, and the outfit you wore to Ascot this year wasn't?"

Nanny Beam chuckled, winking at me.

"You know that I look good in bold colors. In fact, I believe it was you who suggested I experiment with them more in the first place. And anyway, outfits can be removed, as opposed to hair."

"Say what you like, I know you secretly *love* my hair." Nanny Beam grinned.

"I wouldn't change it for the world," the Queen replied. "It's splendid. Or how would the kids describe it these days?"

"I believe something along the lines of . . . 'it's cool!' That means 'marvelous,' doesn't it?" Nanny Beam suggested.

"Yes, very good. Your hair color is *cool*, Nanny Beam!" the Queen said.

They both burst into raucous laughter. I stared at them, my mouth hanging open.

What. Was. Happening.

NANNY BEAM AND THE QUEEN OF

ENGLAND WERE JOKING OVER HAIR AND SLANG. RIGHT IN FRONT OF ME. IN BUCKINGHAM PALACE. AM I ASLEEP RIGHT NOW, I'M NOT SURE.

"Poor Aurora," Nanny Beam said, looking at me and still chuckling. "This must all seem very odd."

"Yes, we have some explaining to do," the Queen admitted, wiping a tear from her eye before collecting herself and turning to me with a serious expression. "Aurora, as you may have guessed, your Nanny Beam and I are old friends."

"Through MI5?" I asked, glancing from one to the other.

"Well, yes, but actually we met before I headed up MI5," Nanny Beam explained. "You mentioned to me that Darek spoke about his father? And what he did?"

I nodded. "He told me he tried to extract

powers from one of the precious stones and in doing so, he was killed."

"That's right. And did he give you any details about that stone?"

"Not really. Just that it was the Jewel of Truth and Nobility. Darek spent years searching for it, but he never found it. He never worked out who its true guardian was or where it was hidden, so he couldn't steal it again and continue his father's work."

"Yes, that's right. The guardian of that stone is only known to the people in this room," Nanny Beam said. "And after we tell you who it is, I expect it to stay that way."

"I promise I won't tell anyone," I said.

"Pinky promise?" the Queen asked, leaning forward and holding out her little finger.

"Pinky promise," I said, wrapping my little finger around hers and shaking it, pretending it wasn't crazily weird that I was making a pinky promise with the Queen.

"Very well." The Queen sat back in her chair. "It's me."

I gaped at her. "You?"

"Yes, me."

She reached over to the wooden box and unclasped it, before entering two codes into locks on either side of it. A robotic voice suddenly came from the box.

"Voice activation."

"Elizabeth," the Queen spoke clearly, as I stared at her in wonder.

A small light on the bottom right of the box went green. The robotic voice spoke again.

"Password."

"Corgis-and-dorgis-forever."

Another green light flashed on the other side of the box.

"Access granted."

The lid released, and the Queen pulled it

up to reveal the grandest, most beautiful, sparkling crown.

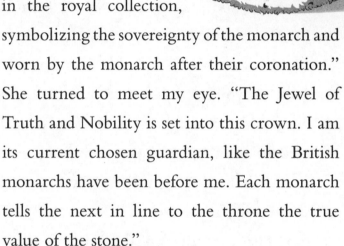

"This is the Imperial State Crown," the Queen said matter-of-factly. "The most magnificent crown in the royal collection, symbolizing the sovereignty of the monarch and worn by the monarch after their coronation." She turned to meet my eye. "The Jewel of Truth and Nobility is set into this crown. I am its current chosen guardian, like the British monarchs have been before me. Each monarch tells the next in line to the throne the true value of the stone."

"I... I don't know what to say," I whispered, my mouth suddenly feeling very dry. "I had no idea."

"Nobody does. Except for your grandmother and me," the Queen explained. "I revealed its true value to her, and only her, when it was stolen from the crown. Together, we managed to keep its disappearance out of the press and then your grandmother discovered it in the warehouse when. . ."

She tailed off and leaned forward to place a comforting hand over one of Nanny Beam's. Nanny Beam smiled weakly.

"I meant it when I said that I understood why you felt you had a duty to return the Light of the World to its rightful place. Like you, I am a guardian of one of these precious stones."

"Is it. . . Is it that big ruby at the front?" I asked, pointing at the crown.

"No. That's the Black Prince's Ruby. It has quite the history, though rather an unfortunate one. You should look it up; it's fascinating. And that there is the Cullinan Diamond, otherwise known as the Second Star of Africa. Beautiful, isn't it? Another stone with an interesting history. And then there's the Stuart Sapphire on the back; very striking. Thought to have been smuggled away by James II when he fled England."

She paused and then raised her hand to the diamond mounted cross at the top of the crown. An octagonal sapphire sat in the center of it. It was smaller than the other stones, but I thought it was the most striking.

"Legend goes that this particular stone was given to a beggar by an ancient king, who had nothing else to give. It was later returned to the crown. It is known as St. Edward's Sapphire." She smiled. "But to the three of us in the room, it is the Jewel of Truth and Nobility."

"Wow," I whispered, unable to take my eyes off it. "It's beautiful."

"And more precious than anyone can know," the Queen commented, before closing the lid gently. There was a sequence of clicks as the locks went back into place.

"Can I ask you something?" I said, continuing when they both nodded. "Why are you telling me about this? It makes sense for you to both know about it – the Queen and its guardian, and then Nanny Beam, you're the head of MI5. But why have you let *me* in on this secret?"

Nanny Beam and the Queen shared a look.

"Because, Lightning Girl," the Queen smiled, "we guardians need to stick together. Don't you think?"

*

"Where have you been?" Georgie asked as I returned to the Bright Sparks. "Fred has managed to fit four cucumber sandwiches in his mouth so far."

Fred tried to say something, but all he managed to do was spray out crumbs. Kimmy was jumping up at him, whining, desperate for him to share.

"He just said 'five,'" Kizzy translated, rolling her eyes. "I keep telling them this is not how you should behave in Buckingham Palace."

"The Queen is back," Suzie said excitedly as we watched her come in, chatting happily with Nanny Beam.

The doors shut behind her, a butler clinked a glass and the room descended into immediate silence.

"What a pleasure and an honor to toast you all today and celebrate your wonderful achievements," the Queen announced, beaming to the sea of faces staring back at her. "I believe it is time to raise a glass and—"

Suddenly, the room was plunged into darkness as the lights all went out, with only a dull light streaming through the windows from the snowy day outside.

"Ah," the Queen chuckled, as her security team instantly surrounded her, "there must have been a power cut. No need for anyone to panic, I'm sure."

"Aurora, help me light the room, would you?" Mum asked, rushing past me and heading toward the Queen.

I took a deep breath, closed my eyes and blocked out everything else. My hands began to glow and then the room lit up in the controlled, soft light beams emanating from my palms.

"Thank you, Lightning Girl," the Queen said, nodding at me.

Nanny Beam had backed toward the door through which she'd just come with the Queen, turned around and was now trying the handle.

"It's locked!" she exclaimed, looking at Mum.

There was a sudden banging noise and the sound of a commotion from beyond the door. Kimmy started barking madly. Everyone in the room gasped and began to talk in panicked whispers.

"Excuse me, Your Majesty," Mum said to the baffled Queen, before ripping a fire extinguisher from the wall and promptly using it to break through the door.

Dad looked at me with a dreamy expression on his face. "Impressive, isn't she, your mum."

As the lock broke from the force of the extinguisher and the doors swung open, Mum raced from the room and I followed, crying, "Come on!" to the rest of the Bright Sparks over my shoulder.

We got out into the corridor to find two security guards and a butler unconscious on the carpeted floor.

"What the—" Mum said, bending down to check that they were OK. "Why would someone do this?"

"The crown," I croaked, a wave of dread hitting me.

Without any further explanation, I raced as

fast as my legs could take me to the small room where the Queen, Nanny Beam and I had been speaking. Mum and the Bright Sparks followed me in hot pursuit.

"Aurora, what's going on?" Suzie yelled as my friends came rushing through the doors.

All the security team and butlers that had been with the Queen earlier were unconscious.

The box containing the crown was gone.

"No."

We spun round to see the Queen standing in the doorway behind us. Nanny Beam put an arm round her. They both looked completely in shock, frozen to the spot at the sight in front of them.

Nanny Beam turned to Agent Holden and was about to give her instructions when we were distracted by the chilling sound of a loud cackle from outside in the courtyard. Kimmy jumped up to rest her paws on the windowsill and began growling at whatever she could see outside.

I ran to the window and peered out, everyone gathering around me to see what was going on. The butler called Joe was wearing the crown on his head and had a jet pack on his back.

"Isn't that the guy who greeted us?" Suzie gasped. "But he was so nice!"

"Joe!" the Queen exclaimed, as Nanny Beam threw open the window. "What are you doing?"

He grinned manically up at us before placing a hand to his face to peel off a prosthetic chin, nose and forehead. He then removed his blond wig to reveal a big, shiny, bald head.

There was a collective gasp from the Bright Sparks.

"MR. MERCURY!" I cried.

"We meet again at last, Lightning Girl! I was worried you might have forgotten me!" Mr. Mercury replied, before offering me a salute.

"Pity it had to be so brief! And don't worry, Your Majesty. I'll look after this precious stone for you. I have wonderful plans for it!"

We watched in horror as he pressed a button on the side of his jet pack and launched himself into the air, disappearing into the sky, the crown firmly on his head, his chilling cackle echoing behind him.

There was a stunned silence.

The Queen slowly turned to address us, her eyes filled with determination.

"Bright Sparks, I know you've just come to the end of one story," she began. "But I wonder if I might trouble you to save the world one more time."

ACKNOWLEDGEMENTS

When I set out on this journey with Aurora Beam I
had no idea how she would be received. I have been
blown away by the love and support for this series – it's
been the greatest ride ever! :) It's a dream come true
to create and work on such a special project. I think
that Aurora Beam is a fantastic role model and symbol-
izes all things good in the world. From being a nervous,
frightened, insecure little girl to growing in confidence,
becoming courageous and wanting to save the world!
She truly is a superhero in every sense of the word and
I love how she learns to embrace what makes
her different and by doing so she inspires others
to do the same!

Some other superheroes that I have the pleasure of working with are listed below. These amazing human beings do extraordinary things to help make Lightning Girl the superstar that she is! Lauren Fortune, Aimee Stewart, Rachel Phillipps, Penelope Daukes, Andrew Biscomb, Rachel Partridge, Eishar Brar and the whole team at Scholastic, Katy Birchall, Lauren Gardner, Steve Simpson, James Lancett & Mike Love! Thank you, thank you, thank you!

To my loyal readers, thank you so much for coming on this journey with me!

May you continue to read and be inspired! Keep shining bright!

Photo by John Wright

ALESHA DIXON first found fame as part of Brit-nominated and Mobo Award-winning group Mis-teeq, which achieved 2 platinum albums and 7 top ten hits, before going on to become a platinum-selling solo artist in her own right. Alesha's appearance on *Strictly Come Dancing* in 2007 led to her winning the series and becoming a judge for three seasons.

Since then she has presented and hosted many UK TV shows including CBBC dance show *Alesha's Street Dance Stars, Children In Need, Sport Relief, Your Face Sounds Familiar* and ITV's *Dance, Dance, Dance*. She is a hugely popular judge on *Britain's Got Talent*.

"My inspiration to create a superhero called Lightning Girl began with wanting my young daughter to feel empowered. It's been a dream to create a strong role model that any child can look up to - I want my readers to see themselves in Aurora, who is dealing with trouble at home and trouble at school alongside her new powers.

I also have a love of precious stones and their healing properties; I have always been fascinated with their spectacular colors and the positive energy that they bring. As human beings we are always searching for something greater within ourselves and a deeper meaning to life and it's my belief that we all have a light within us that can affect change and bring good to the world... we just have to harness it! :)

Enter **AURORA BEAM!**"

Photo by Ian Arnold

Katy Birchall is the author of the side-splittingly funny
The It Girl: Superstar Geek, *The It Girl: Team Awkward*,
The It Girl: Don't Tell the Bridesmaid and the *Hotel Royale*
series, *Secrets of a Teenage Heiress* and *Dramas of a Teenage
Heiress*. Katy also works as a freelance journalist and has
written a non-fiction book, *How to be a Princess: Real-Life
Fairy Tales for Modern Heroines*.

Katy won the 24/7 Theatre Festival Award for Most
Promising New Comedy Writer with her very serious
play about a ninja monkey at a dinner party.

When she isn't busy writing, she is reading biopics of
Jane Austen, daydreaming about being an elf in *The Lord
of the Rings*, or running across a park chasing her rescue
dog, Bono, as he chases his arch nemesis: squirrels.

THE BRIGHT SPARKS

Aurora Beam:
Lightning Girl

Fred Pepe: President
of the Bright Sparks

Cherry Mirella

Benjamin Jackson Jr.
("JJ")

Georgie Taylor:
Stylist

Kizzy Carpenter:
The Brains

Kimmy

Suzie Bravo/Flexi-Girl

(UNBREAKABLE)
PINKY PROMISE!

THE BRIGHT SPARKS
CODE OF CONDUCT

Never let Aurora go on TV again.

1. ~~Keep Aurora's powers TOP SECRET.~~

2. No secrets between members of the Bright Sparks.

3. Never trust a science teacher.

Especially when you are off to meet the Queen.

4. Follow Georgie's fashion advice. ➘

See number 1.

5. ~~Keep Aurora's powers TOP SECRET!!~~

GEORGIE TAYLOR'S GUIDE TO
Fashionably customizing your sunglasses

Do:

 Pair bold colors together, like pink and turquoise, or yellow and orange.

Match your sunglasses to other accessories, like your sneakers.

ADD LOTS OF GLITTER.

Don't:

Pick the safe option – be as imaginative as you can.

 Lose your one-of-a-kind creation (like on the bus...).

 Let anyone tell you what to do!

KIMMY'S
Etiquette GUIDE
FOR MEETING THE
Queen

1. Make sure you have a bath and wear your best bow.

2. Don't chase the Queen's corgis.

3. Let everyone pet you as much as they like.

4. No barking – unless it's at someone who shouldn't be in the palace.

5. Keep an eye on Aurora and follow her everywhere…

READ THEM ALL!